For Fred

First published in Great Britain Collins in 1996
This edition published in 2001
Collins is an imprint of HarperCollins*Publishers* Ltd
77-85 Fulham Palace Road, Hammersmith, London W6 8JB

HarperCollins website address is www.fireandwater.co.uk

1 3 5 7 9 8 6 4 2

Text copyright © Robert Leeson 1996

ISBN 000 710625 4

The author asserts the moral right to be
identified as the author of the work.

Printed and bound in Great Britain by
Omnia Books Limited, Glasgow

Robert Leeson

RED, WHITE & BLUE

Finding out the hard way

An imprint of HarperCollins*Publishers*

RED, WHITE AND BLUE *was originally printed in colour, using: red to show Wain's private letters to an imaginary penpal; white (represented by black typeface on white paper) to show his English project; and blue to show the fantasy story that he is writing. This edition is printed in black and white, but the different chapter headings at the beginning of the sections, as well as the different language used for the letters, the homework and the quest, make it very clear which style Wain is using.*

English Class Seven   The High School
Pen Friend Project   Meadowbank
                                                      Bayfield
                                                         Oxon.

7th September

Hi, I'm Wain.

My real name is Gawain (the one who cut the Green Knight's head off), but mostly I'm called Wain, except by my mother. My brother is called Lance which, as you can guess, is short for Lancelot.

He is five years older than me and a lot bigger. My mother is tall and willowy with green eyes. My grandmother is also tall and stately with white hair. She carries a large blue handbag where she keeps the tablets for my grandfather who is broad and has a red face. They live elsewhere and we see them now and then.

So we are a small family but a big one, if you see what I mean.

Every male in our family for five generations has been a soldier. That is what my grandfather says and he should know. He has a lot of papers about military history and he was very pleased with the new National Curriculum, until they changed it again. I am not sure what he thinks now.

You will notice that I do not mention my father, also very tall, by the way. That is because he is a war hero, or was I mean, in Aden, Anguilla, Belize and Northern Ireland.

But he was missing, believed killed on the shores of the Magellan Strait, south of Rio Gallegos in Argentina. He was leading a raiding party, as a diversion for another raiding party on one of their bases. His party was surrounded, but the other soldiers were able to get away because he covered their retreat. He was never seen again.

That was during the Falklands War and happened before I was born, pretty well. So I have never seen him except in photos. But I know about him from newspaper cuttings. My brother keeps them in a drawer in his room.

When he has finished school and college, he will join the Army and that will make six generations.

In my next letter I'll tell you about my new school, Bayfield High.

22, Croxton Avenue
Bayfield
Oxon., England

9th September

Hi, it's Wain again.

That last lot, on the white paper, was pretty naff, wasn't it. But that was homework. Write to a pen friend or someone and tell them all about yourself.

That's a joke for a start. I don't have a pen friend, or any other sort of friend. We only moved to Bayfield in the summer, and I make friends very, very slowly.

So I'm sorry, friend, but you don't exist. But that is no reason why I shouldn't tell you the whole truth, is it?

This red paper is from a writing set my grandparents gave me when I started High School — red, white and blue writing paper, would you believe?

I was so embarrassed. I know there are some people who wear red, white and blue vests and boxer shorts. That sends my grandfather spare, and makes my grandmother change the subject. But, paper?

Then I had this inspiration. Keep the *white* paper for the *official* version, like homework, which I have to hand in at school, to the powers that be.

Keep the *red* paper for the *real* truth, like when I write to you, unknown friend.

Ah, and the *blue* paper. That's for my *own* writing, for my eyes only — a fantasy novel, about a place called Sylvania. It's so confidential I use a pen name, Gaw Penhallon.

So, let's start again.

First my name. I really like Gawain. But I call myself Wain so as not to attract attention. That is the worst thing you can do in a new school — especially in First Year, I mean Year Seven.

On the white paper I told you ours was a big family. Well, I'm not. I'm vertically challenged, horizontally challenged, diagonally challenged, you name it. I have this weight problem, I don't weigh enough. I read in Biology (which I quite like) that a mature cod is more than a metre long and weighs twenty-eight and a half kilograms. I wouldn't last two rounds with one.

When I was born, my brother was five times as big as

me. Eleven years later and he's still twice as big as me, more or less. I know I'll never catch up, so I'm just hanging on until he joins the Army.

The truth is, my brother's a thug.

When my father... didn't come back, he left some things behind, like a cricket bat, rugby ball and so on. My mother, who is very fair, divided it all up between my brother and me.

But as soon as he could, my brother took everything – I mean every single thing, as well as all the photos and the bits out of the newspapers, up to his room.

He'd have taken Father's medals but my mother keeps those in a case in her room.

I have said nothing about this daylight robbery of my brother's, and it's not out of loyalty. If I did say anything, he would give me a Chinese burn or a kidney punch or lift me up by my hair. I like my hair long, but now I have it cut short just to make things difficult for him.

I keep out of his way and that isn't easy in a small house like ours. I wish we had a big old ramshackle house like my grandparents', with cellars and attics and old cupboards and wardrobes you could disappear into – and maybe never come back.

So, I'm hanging on until my brother leaves home, which is another year, and I have this feeling it is going to be the worst year of my life – so far. I daren't look further ahead.

My brother would have joined the Army already, as a drummer boy or something, but my mother says he has to get his A levels and go to university and then on for a commission. Her father was a brigadier and she expects my brother to aim very high. I've got news for her. He is as thick as two short planks. There is no way he'll get A levels unless he has the answers written on his shirt tail. But I don't reveal my thoughts about him, for obvious reasons – he is very dangerous.

I have a feeling my mother suspects about Lance and the way he is. But I'm supposed to 'stand up for myself' and she won't interfere – unless she thinks he's being unfair – like smearing me all over the cushion covers in the through lounge.

Then she says, quietly, 'You can stop that, Lance!' And, you know, he turns to a jelly when he hears her. You'd better believe it. Those are some of the rare moments of joy in my desperate existence.

But, mostly, to my mother, I'm a disaster area. You see, I do a lot of thinking, about life and that and as a result, I don't *always* notice what is going on round me. I tend to forget things or lose my way.

Mother looks at me, shakes her head. 'Gawain dear,' she says, 'you need an electronic tag,' or 'get a grip on yourself, lad', or worse still, even if she's smiling: 'Gawain, don't be such a big baby.'

Big? If only I were. Baby? I'd vote to go back and start again — if I could start before my father... went. But then, I wasn't here, was I? Maybe if I went back to the future I wouldn't happen second time round.

No, the fact is that I am eleven years of age and nothing but a crisp bag floating on the gutter of life.

Except when I escape to Sylvania, my secret land, where things happen as I want them. There, I'm in charge. So, I'll just finish my homework, first, on the white paper, then get out my special blue paper...

English

Pen Friend Project

The High School

Bayfield

Oxon.

11th September

Hello, Wain here.

   I promised last time I would tell you something of this vexed question of starting a new school – the big school I mean.

   It's a mixture of excitement and fear. Will you get the school of your choice? Will your choice be the right one? You hear all kinds of rumours. School A is really soft, they let you do anything. School B loads you with homework and the staff are like prison warders.

   At School A, they do all sorts of unspeakable things to you, tie you to the goalposts, stick pins in you or throw you in the pond, known popularly as posting, pinning or ponding.

Or they tie your laces together, put glue on your chair, throw eggs and flour over you and put your heard down the toilet and flush it – though not all at the same time.

Or maybe these things happen at School B. You can't be sure. People will tell you anything. Some rumours may have a grain of truth. But then they may not. All you can be sure of is that what you expect will not happen and what you don't expect will.

I can tell you this on my own authority. They call it the big school because everything is bigger and noisier. The students are bigger and noisier and the staff are bigger and make even more noise because they have to.

At your old school you were top of the heap and now you are the bottom. One day there is all the excitement and fun of your last day in Juniors, when you can do what you like. Then in a flash the holidays are gone and you are thrown in at the deep end and no longer know what you can do and what you can't.

Of course if you have a brother or sister at the school that will probably ensure you get a place too and they will be able to tell you things you need to know like which lessons are hard and which are easy, which teachers are strict and which are not.

But at last the big day comes. You're afraid of oversleeping, you check your alarm, change the battery. You can't eat your breakfast. Your new uniform feels like roofing felt. You're afraid of missing the bus and arriving late.

But, amazingly, you get there. You find yourself in a big, crowded hall. Where are the friends you knew in the Juniors? You spot one and wave. But then, names are called and they go through one door, you through another and you don't see them again until break. By then, they are talking to someone else and may not notice you.

But don't worry. There are lots of others in the same boat as you. Beneath those bright smiles, their stomachs may be churning over.

Try to be fair to the school and the school will be fair to you. And remember, by the end of the first year, or even the first term, it will all look different.

SYLVANIA QUEST

Gaw Penhallon

Chapter One
The Death of Anedar

In her island stronghold, at the heart of the once mighty realm of Sylvania, the tall, willowy, green-eyed Queen Sylva sat brooding...

Around her in the throne room of her crystal citadel courtiers, knights, ladies and lords, servants and soldiers waited for her word.

But none came.

No one could read the thoughts behind her haughty, inscrutable expression.

Silently she gazed out over the battlements towards the distant forests and hills of her beloved land, now groaning under the tyranny of Tauro the neighbouring monarch, who only a season ago had invaded peaceful Sylvania with ravening hordes.

Once, in the past, Sylvania had no fear of enemies, no fear of invasion. The serried ranks of its fearless forces had always triumphed in battle.

Their leader, the warrior consort of Sylvania, the hero Anedar, bearer of the magic sword Exordo, was invincible. The man who could defeat Anedar in battle or in single combat had not been born.

But now Anedar was gone, lost in the raging waters of the mighty river which encircled Sylva's palace.

As the grim Tauran cohorts had swarmed across the fertile plains and valleys, the forces of Sylvania were unable to drive them back.

Fighting desperately, led by the great knight Anedar, they retreated step by step, forced to abandon their native land mile by mile until they came to the point of no return, Sylva's stronghold.

There noble Anedar ordered the remnants of his shattered forces to retreat over the massive timber bridge that linked the citadel to the mainland.

Then, while he single-handedly held off with swinging battle axe the ravening ranks of Tauro, he ordered his troops to cut down the bridge behind him, leaving only one slender plank. Then he turned to race along this narrow way. But while the Queen watched in horror, the timber splintered and he fell into the foaming torrent to be carried away into darkness.

Now Sylvania groaned under the heel of Tauro everywhere. Meanwhile in the citadel the Court watched and waited.

At last Sylva drew herself up, green eyes flashing.

'There is only one way to free our noble land. Some knight, some hero must sally forth across the water, find the sword Exordo and defeat our enemies. Or I must submit, marry Tauro and let him rule Sylvania for ever.

'Who will venture forth?'

Hi, for real.

Not bad eh? Written a chapter of 'Sylvania' *and* done my homework. Our English teacher is sneaky. Doesn't set homework, oh no. Just says, 'finish that off at home.' Supposed to make you feel relaxed. She tells me my writing is too 'formal'. This weird character (face like a ferret) who sits next to me warned me to be careful what I wrote down about myself, my impressions of the High. It's a con, he said. Don't trust them. He seems to know a lot and he can whisper without moving his lips. Wish I could. I'm not sure I trust *him*.

But then, I don't trust anyone here.

I've landed up in the same school as my brother, of course. My mother chose the school when we arrived in Bayfield in the summer. She is so used to trolling around from country to country and town to town she can pick out a school just like that.

Number One, she picked Bayfield because it's called 'High'. It's really an old Grammar. It has uniform and the local Compo doesn't. It wouldn't have minded going *there* myself because it's only five minutes down the road from home. Bayfield High is right across town and they hang you up by the thumbs if you're five minutes late. See, I'm spreading rumours already.

What my mother really likes about Bayfield High is the shape of the goalposts, the right game, the right school. Yes, they play rugby. She thinks it's a good, clean, fast game. Little does she know, the mud, the blood, the crunching bones — and it goes on for hours!

Where we lived before, my brother went to a private school. I didn't because there wasn't enough money. Now there isn't enough money for him either, so it's Bayfield High for both of us and he thinks it's the pits. Or he did. Something has changed. What? Wait and see.

I am not bothered. I never wanted to go to private school anyway. You know, in those old school stories they never mention going to the toilet. I used to wonder how my brother managed but I never dared ask.

Bayfield High has toilets. I had a very quick look at them. And that is another false rumour. No one gets their head flushed in the pan because the toilets don't work. The real danger, so my class neighbour says, is passive smoking, after the Year Nines have been in there.

Years Nines are everywhere and to be avoided because they are like something out of *Jurassic Park*. That's another complaint I have about school stories. They are all about Year Nines, never about Year Sevens. I supposed the reason is that Year-Seven life is too painful for fiction.

What else? The food isn't all that bad. I know the refectory resounds to the clang of plateloads of shepherd's pie being dumped in the bins, but I like the shepherd's pie. It sits in your stomach, warm and comforting, and distracts your mind during the long afternoon.

Yes, the teachers. I mentioned English. She is quite pleasant really, not at all sarky. But I shall be careful what I write down. She says that our pieces will be bound up by the Media Department in books and used to encourage children in the junior school. Meanwhile they can be passed round our class to help us get to know each other. I feel a heel not telling the truth on the white paper, but with my Union Jack writing set, I can keep my conscience clear.

Geography's great. I'm good at it which is not surprising, the way our family used to move round the globe. I find maps fascinating. I was the only one in class who knew where the Caicos Islands were. The teacher was impressed but most of the class sneered.

The Games Master looks a real ape. I shall keep out of his way. No good asking my mother for a note to get me excused from PE, etc. She thinks it will make something of me. It will – a nervous wreck.

I've kept the weirdest teacher for last. Our form tutor Mr Sandeman, known as Sandy. He takes Humanities which so far is mainly about Ancient Rome and how much better it was run than this country today. He looks old and wrinkled and it is said he served in World War One, but that can't be right.

Every now and then he has a rant. I'll try and remember this morning's.

'Some misguided people try to tell you school should be fun. It shouldn't. Learning is like aerobics. If it's not hurting it's not doing any good. I know you people, because I taught your parents.

'Most of you are idle and evil and my job is to put that right. I shall fail, but I shall not give up. Various people have tried to make me retire – Authorities, head teachers, pupils. But I shall leave teaching in my own good time. You will not get rid of me so easily.'

'We haven't tried yet,' whispered one smartass at the back of the class. 'I heard that,' rasped Sandy, 'one of the advantages of having a hearing aid. You, my boy, are not the one to do it. I have eaten people like you for breakfast... Right, get your books out and turn to page thirty-six.'

Somehow I feel at home with Sandy. He reminds me of my grandfather without the red face.

The days go by. I still have problems with the timetable, going into the wrong room and being humiliated out of my life. And there is no one I can rely on. I have to make my own way, keeping a low profile.

If my brother was a human being I could ask him. But I keep out of his reach at home and hardly ever see him at school.

But, aha, I did see him the other day, outside the sixth-form block, chatting up this incredible tall girl with long legs and blonde hair. Well, he was trying to, but so were about a dozen other brother lookalikes. It was like those South American tree frogs you see in wildlife films, all those males pushing and shoving to get one female. Nauseating.

Pardon me, I have to go... a long way... back to Sylvania.

SYLVANIA QUEST

Gaw Penhallon

Chapter Two
The Heroes Ride Out

Queen Sylva, beauteous monarch of stricken Sylvania, looked down from her throne at the assembled courtiers, lords and ladies, warriors and servants.

'Who will venture forth fearlessly over the guardian river and search through the land for the lost sword Exordo, our last hope of freedom?'

For a moment there was silence. Then an old man spoke.

'Noble lady, surely this is a hopeless quest. Perhaps our enemies have seized the sword. Perhaps the sword is lost for ever. Perhaps this is a punishment for our wickedness. Perhaps...'

The Queen's eyes were terrible in rage. 'Enough of your perhaps, old fool. Say what you mean: that I should submit to Tauro and offer up our glorious land to shame and degradation.'

The old man shook like a tree in a storm.

'Noble Queen, those were not my words...'

Again the Queen's eyes flashed. 'No, none of you dare say those words, but that is what you all think.'

The throng stood still, aghast and mortified. But in the silence that followed, a tall young man, sword at waist and armour at his broad chest, for he had come at that moment from the jousting yard, strode forward and knelt before Sylva.

'I, Tancelo, son of Anedar, will go. I will venture forth heedless of peril. I will recover Exordo and lead our forces to certain victory. Allow me only to take a few chosen companions. We will leave at dead of night, swimming across the torrent, eluding the dreaded Tauran guards.'

At this a mighty cheer went up to the rafters of the hall. Queen Sylva smiled graciously.

'Tancelo. You will redeem the honour of our realm. Choose your companions.'

But before he could speak another voice was heard. Another young man, slenderly built but handsome, no sword at his side but a parchment roll in his hand, stepped forward.

'I, Ingawa, also son of Anedar, claim the right to ride out with Tancelo.'

There was a moment's hush, then Tancelo laughed and said, 'Not you, Ingawa. You are not for the battlefield. Stay here and write poems.'

The Queen smiled too. 'Yes, Ingawa, you must stay.'

Now the white-haired Queen Mother Grania spoke from the side of the throne. 'Surely the will to fight is what matters. Let Ingawa go.'

But the Queen frowned. 'No, it shall not be. Choose your men, Tancelo.'

That night, Tancelo and six companions rode out, leaving Ingawa to bear his rage and shame.

English Homework

Friendship

The High School

Meadowbank, Bayfield

Oxon.

29th September

Friendship is very important. It can be said that you cannot do without friends, they are an indispensible (?) indispensable feature of a happy life. Where would we be without them?

Let me list the advantages of having friends.

1. You have someone to talk to when you wish to talk about something.
2. Friends help one another in class.
3. Friends stand up for one another, they do not sneak or grass, they do not talk about you behind your back or smirk in a stupid way when you have

made an unfortunate mistake in class,
which anyone could have made.
4. It is fun to mess about together in a
gang.

When you start the new school there is always that difficult time when you lose the friendships you had in the Juniors and have not found anyone you like. You look around the class in the first days and try to work out who, whom you might get to know. Sometimes it seems that everyone else has paired off and you are the only one left.

But be positive. Surely among that crowd of unknown faces there is someone in the same boat as you – looking for a friend?

Do not rush into things. The one who seems friendly may turn out to be untrustworthy. The one you disliked at first sight may turn out to be a friend for life. By the end of term things will seem different.

Once you have made one friend it is easier to make another. But beware of a threesome. That can lead to two ganging up on the third, which is dire. Two is good, four is a gang. A gang is great.

Five or six is a mob, which is mega but not popular with the authorities.

22, Croxton Avenue
Bayfield, Oxon.
Same country

3rd October

Hi, it's Wain, again.

Would you believe it? Miss actually rated my thingey on 'friendship', though in my frank and personal opinion it is a load of garbage, but quite crafty. Still, she says it is observant and mature and who am I to argue? But little does she know.

Since coming to Bayfield High, I have not 'made' a single friend. Mind you, I haven't put myself out to make any. That is a waste of time. The really attractive people, the ones with flair and clout, have already got their crowd. If you try to be friendly they just look amused and turn their back, while one of their hangers-on curries favour by making you look small. Then they all laugh. So I steer clear of all that. It is a lonely life but it saves on humiliation.

So, how come I am the expert on friendship as testified by the English Teacher?

Well, since you are totally discreet (you don't exist) I can tell you the amazing truth. I am the (unacknowledged) leader of a GANG. Yes, me and three friends. I would say 'followers', but that sounds patronizing.

But the brutal fact is that they need me. I can hear you laughing. Need? Me? I have evidence. All three have in the past fortnight attached themselves to me. There must indeed be something magnetic about me.

However, honesty — you are my friend and entitled to the truth — demands I give you the full picture.

The first one to latch on to me was the ferret-faced boy at the next desk. His name is Christopher Ratcliffe and he is nicknamed 'Rat', because he is despised by everyone in the class, except me, because I am not in the despising business. Apart from which I cannot shake him off. I tried moving around and avoiding him, but he just followed me and kept on talking. I tried pretending I was friendly with other people, but he knew I wasn't. There is nothing he does not know, particularly if it is of a sordid nature.

He has the most incredibly dirty mind. He is the chief expert in the school yard on the facts of life. He knows all the theory, which is safer and more fun, I think. I am sure his information is totally wrong but it is absolutely riveting.

For example, he says that if you stand sideways to the bathroom mirror your willie looks longer. Ridiculous of course. But I must confess I tried it out when I went home that afternoon. The first problem is that the only mirror we have is on the cabinet halfway up the wall. I had to balance on the edge of the bath and stretch upwards. And then I couldn't remember how long it had seemed when I looked the time before.

The next member of our gang and the one who actually named it, is Blossom. Yes, she is called Blossom, I kid you not. She's incredible.

She's fat and jolly, with short hair and piercing eyes. She came up to my table in the refectory and just sat down and started to talk. I was gobsmacked when she said she remembered me from Juniors. Why? Because I am a one-parent family and so is she and she thought my mother fantastically beautiful and capable. She has a father.

What else do we have in common? She has a weight problem, like me. If you could amalgamate us you could make up two normal-sized people. Then she does not like sport and wears non-designer and very scruffy trainers for PE. So do I. I wear them because we cannot afford anything expensive. I think her family can afford designer trainers but she won't wear them because everyone else does. And she does not care what she says. It is often unbelievably embarrassing. But she decided that she and I belong together because we are 'misfits'. And so our gang is called Misfits.

We decided that to join, you have to live with just one parent and hate sport.

Then we found out that Rat, of course, had been telling porkies. His mother and father still live together. But he says they don't talk to each other and pass messages through him. And sometimes, to make life more interesting he leaves misleading notes about the house… 'Mum says' or 'Dad does', and then waits for the cosmic row to break out so he can hear them communicating. He's a liar and rotten, but you can't help listening to him.

The fourth Misfit is Graham. He is big and disorganized and always eating slowly and disgustingly. He's always sucking his teeth to get out what is left from his last snack.

He lives with his father and they pig it together at home. I can sort of imagine why his mother left.

His nickname is Soccer, because he is completely football and sports crazy and when he isn't eating he is training to get his weight down, which just makes him hungry again. So why do we let him stay in the gang? Because he is absolutely useless at sport, so incompetent it is a hoot. But he is goalkeeper in one of the local Junior League teams because his father is Chairman of the Committee – and he is very big and very good at football.

And we let Soccer stay because who else would have him if we didn't? The sports fanatics jeer at him and so do the ones with brains – except those in our gang of course.

And one other thing we have in common. Rat says we were all made at the time of the Falklands War. As if I didn't know. He says *he* happened when his mother and father had a reconciliation and were watching British troops landing at Goose Green on the television.

See what I mean?

English Homework   The High School
<u>A Writer in School</u>   Bayfiel

7th October

Today the well-known, in fact famous, writer Kent Farrell visited our school to meet the budding writers of my year. There was tremendous interest in the visit, so much that it was moved from the library to the hall.

Everyone was agog to see the man behind so many best sellers and films. There was much speculation about how he would look, most people thinking that he would be very young and glamorous, very expensively dressed and arrive in a fast Italian car, since he must be a millionaire at least.

In fact he seemed much older, not very sensational and quite friendly. He talked a great deal about when he went to school himself, which was apparently in the

1940s, or maybe it was the 1950s. At any rate it sounded quite like Bayfield High.

He told us some of his Army experiences, when everyone of the right age was made to join. It sounded quite funny, but he said it was very boring, though he had written a book about it.

The way he spoke was indeed often quite amusing. For example, he told us he did not mind if we dropped off to sleep while he was talking as long as we kept our eyes open and fixed on him!

Kent Farrell was of the opinion that school was the most interesting place one could be, in the whole of one's life, if not the happiest, because you had to mix with all sorts of people, whether you liked them or not, which is very true.

After answering questions about his work and his various books – he has written 75! – he read from his latest which will be published next year. It sounded quite interesting.

Then he went on to meet some of the older students. I do not know if he gave them the same talk as he gave Year Seven. It must be rather tiring, but I suppose that is the price of fame.

Since my ambition is to be a writer some day, when I have finished school, I showed him some of the stories which I am now writing – an epic fantasy – to him.

He kindly agreed to look at them and to advise me on where I should get them published.

Kent Farrell is perhaps the most interesting writer I have had the opportunity to meet. I have not met many.

SYLVANIA QUEST

GAW PENHALLON

Chapter Three
A Secret Venture

Months passed. In her citadel, Sylva the green-eyed Queen waited for news of the knight Tancelo and his band. Had they found the magic sword Exordo? Would they rouse the oppressed people of Sylvania to overthrow the tyrant?

But no news came. Only a deep and dismal silence hung over the benighted land.

Ingawa, bitter with rage and humiliation, walked daily on the battlements, looking out over the land groaning under the Tauran heel. His harp hung silent at his side. No longer could he make those poems which once were wont to thrill the Court.

Often he wondered if he would take chance by the forelock and venture out alone. But he bemoaned his lack of skill in arms, for he had no love of war and bloodshed. There seemed no hope.

Till one day as he stood at his post, looking out over the swiftly flowing river, he heard a voice speak behind him.

'My lord Ingawa.'

There stood a man-at-arms, large, broad-shouldered, with a weather-beaten, honest face.

'What do you want, good fellow?' asked Ingawa.

'Sir, I am Maghra and I am of the bodyguard of the Lady Grania. She has sent me to serve you.'

'Serve me? Why and how?'

The soldier came closer and spoke in hushed tones.

'You know that the Lady Grania wishes you to have your heart's desire.'

'Yes,' replied Ingawa bitterly. 'What can I do?'

'My lord. You lack skill in matters of arms. I can train you with sword and axe and bow, in secret. When you are ready you may sally forth.'

'How, alone?'

'No, lord. I shall ride at your back and fight with you, to the death.'

A broad smile came over Ingawa's gentle, handsome face.

'I thank you, Maghra, and shall reward you.'

'I need no reward,' answered the honest warrior, 'except to help you find the magic sword and free our beloved country.'

And so Ingawa put aside the harp and the parchment and turned in secret to arts of war, until the day came when in mid-combat, Maghra said: 'Lord, I can teach you no more. Say the word and we shall go forth.'

'Very well,' answered the minstrel prince. 'Tonight, be ready. We shall travel on foot disguised as wanderers, I a minstrel, you my companion. Our weapons must be hidden and you must not say my name. None must know who we are until we find Exordo.'

That night, Prince Ingawa and his faithful retainer swam across the torrent and vanished into the Sylvanian forests.

22, Croxton Avenue
Bayfield

9th October

Guess who... Your old pal Wain!

For once I was sorely tempted to put down the real truth about that writer visit, even in my homework, on white paper. I was so disgusted. It was dire.

But Rat said: 'Cool it. Suppose they send all the stuff to Kent Farrell, like feedback.' He has a terrible view of life, always expecting the worst. But he is usually right and I would not like Kent Farrell to see this.

As I said, the visit was a shambles. It could have been major, the way it was supposed to be. There were going to be about twenty of us, the ones really into creative writing, in the library, for a workshop session.

Then some clown said that was elitist and they asked him if he would talk to all Year Seven. And he agreed! Suicidal. So instead of a quiet hour in the peace of the library we have a scrum in the hall, made even more chaotic by 7H who turned up late and clambered over everyone else.

Guess who were the worst? The girls, the more developed ones that is. They shoved up to the front, took over the whole row and sat there crossing and uncrossing their legs, trying to look sexy and quite frankly looking stupid.

It turned out later that they thought he might be talent-spotting young stars for the film of his latest book. When Kent Farrell told them he had nothing to do with studio production, they went right off him.

In fact they started going off him the moment he came into the hall, carrying this pile of papers and books which he dropped. They must have been expecting a cross between a rock star and Captain Kirk but he was just ordinary – going a bit thin on top and so on.

I quite liked him. He was friendly. Right away he said, relax, go to sleep if you like as long as you keep your eyes open. That got a laugh, until the chimps from 7H started making rhythmic snoring noises.

Blossom was sitting next to me and I heard her whisper, 'This is so embarrassing.'

Then Sandeman, who had been sitting at the side suddenly got up, took two of the chief snorers by the ears and led them out — well, slung them out. Kent Farrell, I thought, looked a bit peeved but it quietened down and he started to talk.

Everyone has it in them to write, but it has to be enjoyable. It has to be fun. I could see Sandy glowering at that word.

School was the place to get ideas, he said (some joker at the back started to snigger, I can guess what ideas he had in mind), and characters, too. 'Look around you. Every class contains enough characters for a dozen novels.'

What happened? Of course, they had to start looking round and pointing and making stupid faces, till Sandy stood up and quelled them again.

Everybody listened, though, when Kent talked about his days in the Army as a teenage conscript and how he had decided to write the truth about it, so blokes wouldn't be lured into joining by TV reports of the Falklands and the Gulf War.

Suddenly, I thought — suppose somebody had turned my father off the Army? He might still be around today. But would he have listened? My brother wouldn't.

There were the usual questions. How does it feel to be a millionaire? He said he wasn't, but I don't think they believed him. Do you work at night? Do you use a word processor? Have you written any horror stories? Any football stories?

He was so patient. He didn't seem to notice when some idiot asked a question he'd answered five minutes before. He didn't even seem to notice when they started yawning and shuffling at the back. He just went on talking — and looking at the clock now and then.

Then something totally amazing happened. Somebody asked him where he got all his ideas from and he started to answer. 'As I said before, keep your eyes open, be aware of the people round you. Whether it is fantasy stories, school stories or thrillers or comic stories you intend to write, it is all about people… Observe closely and try to understand those immediately round you. Knowing what makes people tick is half the business of writing…'

While he was talking I could hear Blossom making strange sighing noises. All of a sudden she started giggling, then she burst out laughing, uncontrollably.

Kent Farrell stopped, turned red and glowered at her. She tried to stop, but started coughing, then hiccuping. Everybody was looking at her and they were starting to laugh and cheer.

Up got Sandy. 'I think you had better do that outside, miss,' he said in his usual rasping way.

Blossom staggered up and ran out. There was dead silence for a bit, then Kent Farrell very quickly opened a book and began to read aloud.

He hadn't finished the story when the buzzer went. He gathered all his papers and struggled out while Sandy was making everybody give him a round of applause.

I just had time to get to the door first and stopped him to ask if he could look at my Sylvania stories. He looked at me, a bit wildly, I thought, but then he made a thin sort of smile and took my folder.

In lunch break I looked for Blossom, but she seemed to have been excused and gone home. Next day she didn't want to talk about it and I didn't ask.

Rat told me I was wasting my time giving Kent Farrell my stories. 'You'll be lucky if he even writes back. He must get thousands of things sent to him.'

Make me happy!

As I was going home I suddenly realized two things. One was I'd given Kent Farrell the only copy of 'Sylvania Quest'. And the other was it didn't have my real name on, just Gaw Penhallon.

SYLVANIA QUEST

Gaw Penhallon

Chapter Four
Enter Dearna

Ingawa and his loyal retainer Maghra vanished from the citadel in search of the magic sword Exordo. When she discovered that the young prince had disobeyed her and gone, the green-eyed Queen Sylva was furious with rage. Her anger was awesome to behold. But Grania, the gracious white-haired Queen Mother, smiled a secret smile.

Meanwhile the two adventurers made their way by forest paths and little known tracks, skilfully evading the patrolling Tauran soldiers.

In each village they made discreet enquiries in the faint hope that some rumour, some clue might be revealed that would lead them to the Magic Sword. But folk refused even to speak of it, their eyes rolling in terror.

From this Ingawa knew that Tauro the brutal tyrant was also looking for the sword and had not found it. But then nor had the mighty Tancelo of whom there were also no tidings.

Some said they thought he was in the mountains to the north, or in the marshes of the south. But no one knew. He had vanished utterly with his band of warriors.

In each village where they passed the night, Ingawa would tell tales to earn their supper. They were always welcome were the two wanderers in their rough peasant clothes.

But one evening, while Ingawa was busy with his story-telling, the watchful Maghra spotted a lean, dark figure in the background, his nimble fingers prying amid the bundles the two travellers carried with them.

In one bound the soldier seized the thief.

'Dog, I'll break your arm,' he swore. The thief, his face and nose thin and rat-like, wriggled in Maghra's grasp.

'I beg you, let me go. I am just a humble wayfarer looking for a crust.' His voice quavered. 'I am so hungry...'

'I'll cut your throat, then you'll never be hungry again,' rasped Maghra.

Hearing their voices, Prince Ingawa hastened to intervene.

'Who are you?' he demanded.

'I am called Rodon.'

'A good name,' said Ingawa. 'You ought to be thrashed but I will let you go.'

'No, let me follow you, lord.'

Ingawa frowned. 'What do you mean, Lord? I am a minstrel.'

Rodon shook his head. 'No, no. The weapons in your bundle show you come from the citadel. I heard you ask about the magic sword. I can help you.'

'How?'

Rodon tapped his nose. 'There is a minstrel abroad in the land called Dearna. He tells about the sword Exordo and promises it will strike again. If any soldier tries to arrest him, he vanishes.'

Maghra shook his head. 'Don't trust him.'

But Ingawa said, 'Lead us to Dearna.'

English   The High School

<u>Pen Friend Project</u>   Meadowbank, Bayfield

                                            Oxon.

                                       13th October

Hello again.

    Your first five weeks in the new school have passed and it is time to take a look round and ask: how has it been? The answer will probably be, not as bad as I feared.

    You have discovered which lessons you like and which you dislike. I quite like English, Geography is great, History too, in a way, Science, good and not so good, Humanities, sort of unusual, Maths a disaster area and Games/PE, an ordeal. But then I am opposed to compulsory physical exercise since it can lead to becoming muscle-bound in later life.

You have discovered the armoury of weapons or shall we say the menu of punishments which the powers-that-be have on offer, or at their disposal. There are detentions, of course, infuriating when individual, but quite entertaining when handed out en masse.

There are lines. Yes, these are in fashion again, because of their power to drive the victim spare by their sheer inconvenience. Extra homework should be included here, although teachers who handed it out may be under the delusion that they are helping you.

The Games/PE teacher has his own special menu of press-ups, running round the field, etc.

Then we have being thrown out of class, being sent to Mr Holcroft, and as a last resort, the Boss and the Big C, or cane, known chiefly by rumour.

If all else fails, there are suspension and expulsion. My friend Christopher remarks that since you are made to go to school by law, it is odd to punish you by throwing you out. But the ways of the adult world are not to be questioned.

Some punishments can give you a reputation and this will help you survive in class. If you cannot get a rep, then the best protection is third-party insurance, always have a witness, someone to speak up for you, a friend, in fact. Otherwise your only hope is to keep a low profile.

However, keeping a low profile may not save you from the ultimate horror – sarcasm. Anyone who is not concrete from ear to ear fears the sarcastic teacher, more than the strict one.

Sarcasm exposes you to the scorn and derision of the mob in classroom, corridor or worst of all, the playing field.

Punishments may be forgotten, embarrassment and humiliation, never!

At home!!

16th October

Hi.

What do you know? Ms Redmond thought my 'letter'
on crime and punishment was pretty good. I have to
agree. It was written with feeling. I was nearly carried
away and revealed all because in recent days I have
endured cosmic humiliation. I have to tell someone,
though now I cannot trust anyone, least of all myself.

I gave chapters of 'Sylvania' to Kent Farrell since I
was sure he would rush them to his publisher. But how
would he get in touch with me? All he had was my pen
name. I lay awake at night, thinking: he'll ask the school
who is this Gaw Penhallon? If the mob knew my pen
name I would melt down and leak away.

I even hoped Rat was right and Kent would sling my

stuff in the bin. But that could be worse than ridicule and contempt – I think.

Then a big envelope arrived for me, at home! Out fell my Sylvania story plus some notepaper headed 'Kent Farrell'. His letter (typed) was friendly. He gave me tips on plot development and urged me to press on. Nothing about a publisher though.

Phew! I realized he probably rang the school and asked who was that intelligent and sensitive boy who spoke to me as I walked out on that bunch of savages in the hall that day?

Then I shook the big envelope again. Out fell a smaller one. Inside more notepaper, with a few words in pencil. It said: 'This is great stuff. I think the realist mode suits you better than fantasy. But I don't think you'd like to have it published. Good luck.

'P.S. I shall not reveal your pen name to anyone. I like my own name to be secret.'

Inside the envelope were four sheets of red paper, about the Misfits and teachers. I must have stuck them in with the blue sheets.

You think that's dire. Wait for Cringe No. 2.

My mother took me to the doctor's. She thinks I look peaky and why don't I grow upwards and outwards? The doctor said I'd probably 'shoot' up later on. He suggested a tonic and, wait for it, yeast tablets.

Have you any idea (a) what they taste like? (b) what effect they have? People started looking at me, pointing, even moving their desks. I appealed to my mother but she just laughed and said: 'Give it a week and your tum will settle down.'

How many days' humiliation can one human being take? I was a laughing stock. But several teachers jumped to the totally false conclusion that I was doing it on purpose, to get a rep in class.

I got a hundred lines (apiece) from four teachers in one day: 'I must not disrupt the class' or some such. I was desperate. Four hundred lines and homework as well.

So, picture me, late one afternoon sneaking into the computer room with the crazy idea of doing them on the word processor.

I had no idea how to work one, nor even how to start it. Fortunately there were no staff around. I couldn't ask them for help.

Then in wandered this sixth former, big, plump, untidy, with floppy fair hair. He asked me what my problem was and was so friendly, I told him. He almost creased with laughter, and I had to join in.

He set the machine up for me. But my mind went blank about what I was supposed to write. So he improvised. By this time, it was too late to care. The lines had to be in the next day, and I was laughing so much I was getting hysterical.

'I must not fart in Maths/Biology.' And, personalized for Mr Sandeman, 'I must not break wind in Humanities.' Then, when it came to 'I must not fart in French,' he said: 'How do you fart in French?' he thought a bit: 'It must be like *partir*: *Je ne dois pas fartir en Français.*' By this time I was nearly rolling on the floor.

When it was all done, he said: 'You're Lance's kid brother aren't you? You're mad on writing.' I was gobsmacked but he went on: 'I'm Keith. Drop in again. We'll put your stories on disks. It's OK, I've got the run of this place.'

The crazy thing was the computerized lines worked. The French teacher even laughed. But Sandy gave me a fierce look and said: 'Wain boy, lines are meant to be labour intensive, not high-tech. Write them out again by hand.' But he wasn't angry.

Then something happened. Not embarrassing, weird.

I called into the computer room now and then. Keith Clarridge read my stories, and made some suggestions. We talked about ourselves. He is so easy to talk to, like there was no age difference.

He was brought up by his gran. He understands how I feel about never seeing my father, as though he were lost somewhere in the sea and sky. Keith said: 'Suppose your dad were still alive? They never found his body. Who knows, he might be still there.'

'What, in Argentina?'

'Stranger things have happened.'

That evening Lance was out. Trolling round after that blonde I expect. I sneaked into his room, got the newspaper cuttings out of the drawer and was reading through them when he crashed in.

'What the hell are you doing, you little…?'

I gabbled something about wondering if my father was still alive.

He went red. 'What, living with the bloody Argies?' He grabbed my shirt front.

'Who's been putting that idea in your stupid head?'

'Keith Clarridge.' I was stuttering.

He turned puce. 'Clarridge? You stay away from him. What's he want, messing about with kids?'

Just then, my mother called out: 'What's all the row, boys?' And came into the room. Lance went quiet. When he spoke, his voice was very small.

'He's going on about Daddy, gone over to the Argies.'

My mother looked at us both, then said; 'I'm sure he didn't mean anything like that. Did you?' I couldn't speak. I shook my head. 'Gawain has a little too much imagination.'

She reached out, ruffled my hair. Lance barged out and slammed the door.

The weirdest thing was, that night I dreamt we moved and lived in the same house as Kent Farrell.

English Essay   The High School
<u>Bullying</u>   Bayfield, Oxon.

                                          20th October

Bullying is very fashionable these days. I mean it is getting a lot of exposure on the media. This is a good thing. But what will happen when they get tired of it and move on to something else? Bullying will still be there.

It always has been. It is as much a part of school life as shepherd's pie in the refectory. It goes on so much that even the victims don't know it. They think this is how people, even friends, behave to one another and if it stopped, they would think something was wrong with them.

Friends? I hear you ask. Yes, an awful lot of bullying goes on between friends – or people in the same set, like long-term loans of things and money. If you object, you're out.

Another thing is that bullies get bullied. It's like the food chain in those nature films – eat or be eaten. And it's not just big people bullying smaller ones. Very often the bully isn't bigger, but is just prepared to go farther and do nastier things.

It's all a matter of willpower. If you show you can be just as unpleasant, they lose interest. But who wants to live like that?

In those old school stories, the hero fights the bully behind the school gym and always wins? Why? Because the bully always fights fair, and he's a coward which helps. But what would happen if three of them got you behind the bike sheds or waited for you after school? There's not much you can do then, is there?

Those schools, and there are a lot of them, who say, 'Oh, we don't have bullying, just the general rough and tumble, the kids sorting it out between them, a bit like an assault course in the Army,' are so wrong.

Of course the school doesn't find out because the victim does the honourable thing and never grasses.

The mob is more to be feared than the staff because the staff are controlled by rules, but the mob makes its own rules.

So, you either keep a low profile, like be invisible, or you get your own gang, or you become a champion sprinter and hurdler. Or all three.

SYLVANIA QUEST

Gaw Penhallon

Chapter Five
The Taurans Strike

So the companions, now three in number, Ingawa, his loyal retainer Maghra and the cutpurse Rodon, set off in their search for Dearna, the mysterious minstrel.

As they journeyed, through forest and heath, over hill and dale, in rocky places and swampy lowlands, Ingawa and Maghra kept a close eye on the third member of their band. To be frank they did not trust him. He was a liar and a thief.

His saving grace was that he told them the truth, at least, and, after the first night, did not attempt to rob them. But his 'skills' did not remain idle: all sorts of game, fish and fowl appeared in their travelling larder as if by magic, so that the previous owners had no knowledge of their loss.

And when the little group of wayfarers was stopped by heavily armed Tauran patrols, Rodon's sharp wit and slippery way of talking extracted them from tight corners, time and again.

So they journeyed on, into the heart of Sylvania and closer to the towns where the main Tauran forces had camped. More and more on the highways they met the occupiers, and more and more Rodon's dubious skills were needed.

But as they travelled into the heart of enemy territory, so they came closer to the trail of Dearna the wandering minstrel.

Where he had been the villages were alight with his message. A new spirit seemed to be abroad. The mood of despair was lifted. It was marvellous to hear how talk of a sword could raise people's hopes. What more could be done with the sword itself?

One day they marched into a little town. It was market day and the square was crowded but no one was buying and selling. They were listening to a hooded figure whose face was invisible. His voice, rich and deep, told a strange and wonderful tale.

'The sword Exordo will shine again, when the warrior fit to wield it comes among us.'

Now the crowd began to mutter and applaud. 'Tell more, Dearna,' they called.

'I will tell you this. When that warrior comes, and no one will know until he comes, the sword will strike and Sylvania's enemies will fall.'

The cheers were interrupted by a brutal voice. There on horseback sat a Tauran patrol, eight heavily armed soldiers with a huge bearded captain.

'Who are these enemies, storyteller? Speak!'

But the cowled figure said nothing.

'Very well, minstrel. You shall answer at the end of a rope. Seize him.'

But before the soldiers could move, Ingawa held up his hand.

'Wait sir. This man is but a storyteller. His words are not meant to harm anyone. Do not punish him.'

'Who are you, little man?'

'Just a traveller.'

'Well, traveller, you shall hang in the place of the minstrel,' growled the Tauran captain.

Ingawa turned. The space where the minstrel Dearna stood was empty.

'Seize the boy,' commanded the Tauran.

22, Croxton, etc.

22nd October

Phew!

Life is getting very complicated. Just as some things seem clearer, others get more mysterious. Let me tell you. Well, you can't stop me, can you? That is what I like about you, you are such a good listener.

My essay on bullying was a hit. Ms Redmond said it was well thought out, though it showed a sad view of life in one so young.

Young I may be but I have long experience of bullying. I was brought up on it. It is supposed to make a man of you. Well, in my case it is taking a very long time.

That is at home, I hasten to add. At school I have seen a lot of it going on. I have a good eye for it, even when it's done on the sly like a lot of bullying is.

But, I'll be honest, I haven't suffered all that much. Or I hadn't until this very day. And more of that in one moment.

The reason for my charmed life is that in the early days I kept a low profile (home training). And then within *weeks* of starting school I assembled this brilliant outfit around me, the Misfits. Together we are quite – impressive.

Take Soccer now. I know that he is quite useless at his chosen sport of football and is a standing joke which, to give him his due, he takes very well.

But he is big and has the kind of large, dim face that can look quite menacing when he frowns. That is usually because he is bewildered, not because he is uptight. In fact he almost never gets narky, and that is one reason why I like him, despite his disgusting eating habits.

Then, there is Rat. He is completely unreliable, so unreliable you can depend on him. He will desert the ship even when it is not sinking. Self-preservation is his great talent. But he is cunning and well informed and thus the Misfits have an early warning system for possible aggro. And, when cornered, he can talk himself and his friends out of trouble.

The truly amazing one, though, is Blossom. Being a girl and overweight she ought to be miserable and sorry for herself. But not on your nelly. She does not give a toss for anything or anybody.

The only time I can remember her being at a loss was on the famous day when Kent Farrell the writer came to Bayfield High and she had this sudden fit of hysterics.

She has never explained to me or anyone else why it happened and I haven't wanted to pry. It is just one of those mysteries I mentioned to you at the beginning.

This is all leading up to what I promised to tell you about — being bullied, at school. It was weird, it was alarming and it was totally baffling.

At lunch break Soccer was off training somewhere (on a full stomach, the idiot, but then he can't do anything on an empty one). Rat and I were trolling around chatting about this and that and wondering where Blossom had got to.

Then we found her, on the grass slope above the pond. No one knows why the school has a pond and it is fenced off and strictly *verboten*. People are alleged to be ponded or thrown in fully dressed, but I have never seen this happen and probably never will.

She wasn't alone. She was talking to a sixth former, and not just any sixth former, but Oldfield, star rugby forward, built like a brick wall and awesomely evil, making my brother look like a Samaritan.

He was pushing something at her, a piece of paper, an envelope or something. And she was shaking her head. She didn't seem bothered. But he was. He got so wound up, he shoved the paper at her saying something like 'go on', and she couldn't help it. She jerked back.

My family genes must have taken charge. I didn't do it on purpose. But I stepped up and said something really embarrassing, like 'Leave her alone'.

He turned round. His big meaty face screwed up. I could see his small brain working. He'd found someone he could take it out on. He grabbed me. My feet left the ground. He said, 'Don't you stick your nose in my business, you little poof.' I could feel the blood leaving my body, when Blossom said:

'Leave him alone or…'

And he let me go. She reached out, took the paper from him and stuck it in her blazer pocket. Oldfield walked off but as he did, he snarled at me: 'I'll get you for this, you little ponce.'

We three stood there gobsmacked for a second or two. Then I asked her: 'What was all that about?' but she shook her head and answered: 'Private.' Then she punched me on the arm.

'You're an idiot. Fancy telling him to leave me alone. He could eat you.'

'But you told him to leave me alone,' I said.

She smiled, a bit craftily. 'That's different.' Then she frowned. 'Why was he so, but so, insulting to you? It wasn't as though you could do anything. And what's all this "poof" business?'

Rat put a finger to his nose: 'I know. I meant to say something to you Wain, but I didn't like to.'

'Like what?'

'You are friends with Clarrie, aren't you?'

'Who?'

'You can't be that dim, Wain. Keith Clarridge. I've seen you with him outside the computer block.'

I was baffled. 'So? He's been putting my stories on disk. He's OK, not like a lot of sixth formers, treat you like dirt.'

Rat shook his head as though he pitied me. 'You are so naive. Everybody knows Keith Clarridge is gay. That's why they call him Clarrie.'

All of a sudden I remembered how my brother had gone spare over Keith. 'But, Keith's never...' I began.

'Course he hasn't,' said Rat. 'Like you say, he's OK. He's got a friend in the Sixth at the Compo. But you know what dirty minds people like Oldie have, Wain. You want to watch it mate.'

SYLVANIA QUEST

Gaw Penhallon

Chapter Six
The First Battle

The Tauran warriors set spurs to their steeds, scattering the hapless men and women in the market square. In that instant Ingawa saw that further concealment was useless.

'Let us defend ourselves!' he called to Maghra. In one movement, prince and servant drew their swords from the bundles on their backs. As one they swung, their keen blades burning in the sunlight, and the first two Tauran riders reeled from the saddle, to fall like stones into the dust, their lifeblood gushing out.

'Ride them down,' bellowed the Tauran leader. Now the patrol drew back to gain space, unslung their lances and wheeled about. As the crowd scattered, a row of steel points aimed at the gallant two. Rodon, crafty as ever, had vanished among the throng.

'Charge!' came the command and the crowd began to scream and run as the horsemen bore down. But before they had gone three paces, a girl's voice called:

'Sylvanians! Do not let brave men die alone.'

At the sound of her words, the charging horsemen hesitated in their onward stride.

As they did, the speaker, a stocky, round-faced peasant girl stooped and swept up stones into the fold of her skirt. Around her, youths and old women did the same.

'Charge!' came the command once more and the horses sprang forward. But before the lance points could pierce the flesh of our two companions, a hail of stones and market filth fell on their heads and shoulders.

Three riders fell from their saddles. The others swung round in confusion, their horses neighing in fright. Ingawa and Maghra leapt forward, blades thrusting upwards. Down went two more Taurans and before the other soldiers could pull away the crowd rushed forward, dragged them from their mounts and beat them to death.

The noise and turmoil were hushed. The battle of the marketplace was over. The Taurans lay still, their horses pawed the ground, riderless.

Ingawa leapt upon the platform where the storyteller had stood.

'Seize their weapons.'

Then he turned to the older people and ordered: 'Get ready your families to march into the forest.'

The girl with the stones called out.

'Run away?'

Ingawa responded indignantly: 'No, to prepare for our first real battle when their comrades in arms return to punish this town. Tell me. What is your name?'

'Blodwen,' answered the girl proudly. 'Stranger, what is *your* name?'

Drawing himself up, he answered with equal pride: 'I am Ingawa, youngest son of Anedar.'

As the square rang with cheers, Rodon suddenly spoke at Ingawa's elbow.

'That was not wise, to shed your disguise, my lord.'

Ingawa replied haughtily: 'The time for disguise is over.'

English Essay   The High School
<u>Competitive Sport:</u>   Bayfield, Oxon.
<u>Is it a good thing?</u>

27th October

The first question one ought to ask is: Is sport a good thing, full stop?

And the answer for any thinking person must be 'no'. I hasten to add that I am not against exercise. I like walking, with a friend or a not-too-energetic dog.

I refer, of course, to PE and sport, the compulsory and violent inflicting of unwanted, dangerous physical activity on the human frame.

This is wrong in the first place because it puts the intelligent person to the unwanted attentions of the stupid – if they happen to be larger and more muscular – as is often the case.

Anyone who believes sport can develop the mind has only to think about retired boxers who wander round making aimless gestures with their fists.

Or, for example, one of those television programmes about champion athletes who develop arthritis and similar in later life.

Of course, one does not have to wait for later life to suffer indignity and injury.

This can happen on, for example, the rugby pitch, ranging from having one's shorts pulled off to bruises, cuts, bleeding noses and broken bones.

There is much indignation about blood sports. But this is only where animals are involved. Are not human beings entitled to protection from those who have the urge to pursue, persecute and physically molest?

Let us face the truth. Sport is just a lawful kind of bullying.

So far I have spoken only of non-competitive sport. Competitive sport is even more repulsive because it brings out the worst not only in the players but also in the spectators.

The spectators, at ringside, or in grandstand, or even in the armchair in front of the square screen, incite the players to foul play and violence.

If there is not enough of the latter on the field, then

the said 'fans' indulge in orgies of foul play and violence in the streets afterwards. Sportsmanship?

And this is supposed to develop the mental, moral and physical wellbeing of young people? I rest my case.

22, Croxton, etc. etc.

30th October

Well, well.

I had hoped to repeat the triumph of my thingey on bullying with my splendid attack on sport. But Miss marked me down and wrote at the bottom, 'Gross exaggeration does not help your case.'

Sometimes I think the more sensitive members of the staff just close their eyes to what goes on in the gym, on the rugger pitch or worse still in the changing rooms. The inhumanity of one living creature to another. I can't describe some of these people as human.

And the one who ought to uphold law and order, ensure fair play and protect human rights, the one who pretends to be referee during these bouts of mud wrestling which are called 'games' – he is the worst of all.

His signature on detention slips is A.P. Earnshaw, so naturally he is known as APE. His parents when they named him must have guessed how he would turn out. I cannot believe any church would baptize him. While most teachers either do not know or pretend they do not know their nicknames, Ape glories in his.

If there were trees along the touchline he would swing from branch to branch, howling, 'Keep it in play, you little squit.' His language, as well as being gross, is terribly out of date.

He is cosmically insensitive. Once during a particularly gruesome match, one boy let out an agonized yell, 'Leggo my balls.' What do you think Ape did? He just grinned and shouted: 'Mind your language in the scrum.'

His sense of humour, like that of all muscle men, is abysmal. But he thinks he is terribly witty. When he discovered my full name, for at least a fortnight he greeted me with 'Hurry up! Are you coming or Gawain?' You see what I mean.

Only Rat, my friend, is a match for him. Once in the gym Rat was in some discomfort after a misjudged vault over the horse (if there is one thing I hate more than the horse, it is the box, or the beam or the parallel bars, or the ropes...).

Anyway, Ape bawls at Rat: 'What's up with you, lad — got a ferret in your trousers?' to which Rat replied like a flash: 'No, sir, just the usual sensitive parts.' Ape was speechless.

The chief target of Ape's vileness is in fact our pal Soccer, who cannot get it into his head that the official school game is rugby. He *will* dribble the ball, at least he tries to. But since he is not brilliant with a round one, he is dire with an oval one.

'Pick it up, you clown,' yells Ape. At the third offence, Soccer is sentenced to press-ups or running round the field and of course he spends most of the game off the pitch.

Yet Soccer never grumbles and he never gives up. I admire him. That sounds strange but I do admire people who are single-minded. I am always in three minds at once which helps in writing but not in life.

I never know how I appear to other people. One day Mr Sandeman stopped me as I was going home and said (I remember his words very clearly):

'Wain, you are the sort of boy who gets into hot water when he doesn't mean to. You are really shy and retiring, but you keep saying and doing things that give the wrong impression. If I did not know otherwise I would say you are a little stirrer. Just watch it.'

Where was I? Soccer. He is a good friend and right now he is helping me with my No. 1 problem — how to stay out of the reach of that animal Oldfield.

For some reason I cannot work out, I am safe while I am with Blossom. But what about the other times and places where Blossom cannot be present, and Oldie may appear? Apart from which it is beneath my dignity to hide behind her all the time, although, considering her size and mine, I could do that quite easily.

One day he will find me on my own. And then... Despite what I have said about sport, I toyed with the idea of becoming a karate Black Belt in order to destroy him. But I believe it takes years, while I have only weeks — if I am lucky.

I also thought of putting pins in a wax image on Hallowe'en at the weekend. Do I want him to die in agony? Yes. But will it work?

The last option is training to run faster than Oldfield. So I am up at the crack of dawn each day jogging with Soccer. Getting up is the pits but once through the park and trotting up Baybury Hill, I actually feel *good*.

We don't strain ourselves. At the top, Soccer stops for a pre-breakfast which he carries in a rucksack, a couple of large sausage rolls or four-tier burgers, which he generously shares with me.

Sometimes we sit and chat about the weird characters (ourselves excluded) who go jogging in the park. Or we just sit, like friends, in silence.

I expect he thinks about scoring the winning goal in the World Cup (when we get into the final).

But I brood on questions I cannot answer like: why is Oldie so careful when Blossom is around?

Or why do people like him hate blokes like Keith Clarridge, who wouldn't harm a fly and just want to help others?

Most of all, why would my brother rather imagine my father dead than alive and living in Argentina? I would quite like to think of him as living and breathing, not just a picture and a leather case full of medals and a bunch of yellow bits of newspaper.

Now something I kept till last. This morning as I got up to go out with Soccer, I found a letter addressed to my mother on the mat. I had a quick look at it before I heard her on the stairs.

The envelope was flimsy, like airmail. The stamp was foreign. The postmark was very blurred, but I could just make out three bits of words, Buen… ires… Arg…

English Essay   The High School
My Half-Term Holiday   Bayfield, Oxon.

1st November

I spent half term with my grandparents, or, to be more exact, with my grandmother, because my grandfather is usually at the golf club. My mother dispatches me to Grandmother's sometimes when she feels the need to get out of the house – which I also feel sometimes.

Grandmother likes to cook, which my mother isn't at all keen on. So I spend a lot of time in the kitchen watching her and talking. Well, she talks and I listen.

In the kitchen jugs and bowls are covered up with cloths that have beads round them. This is a habit from living in hot countries where germs and creepy-crawlies fall into the food.

Their house is big and old and is full of pots and brass things which Grandmother bought in the market in India or Aden or Egypt or elsewhere. She always liked to go into the bazaars and bargain for 'bits and bobs' as she calls them. Some of the other officers' wives though this was a bit off, but she didn't mind.

We also went on long walks during the week, very slow ones because their dog Winston, which is a bulldog, believe it or not, is very, very old, a good bit older than me.

She told me all sorts of things she remembered. For example, they were in Egypt during the big cholera epidemic which was about fifty years ago. Thousands of Egyptians died, but no British troops. They just ate all their bread toasted, dipped their eating irons in boiling water and had a saltwater injection.

Grandmother and Grandfather have been all over the world, from one end to another. They got married in 1943. My grandfather joined the Army as a boy soldier and became a major. My grandmother was a colonel's daughter.

Their son (my father that is, or was) was born just after they left India. When he started school they were just leaving Egypt. When he was my age they lived in Guyana and Belize. Sometimes he was with them and sometimes he was in England, at school.

When he grew up he joined the Army and became a captain. He married a brigadier's daughter (that is my mother, of course).

I suppose that when my brother joins the Army he should marry a general's daughter. But my Grandmother thinks there will not be enough generals' daughters to go round by then.

SYLVANIA QUEST

Gaw Penhallon

Chapter Seven
The Sword

That day and the night which followed the townsfolk lay hidden with their children in the depths of the forest.

The town lay empty save for a few scouts whom Ingawa had posted at the edges to watch the road in either direction.

Sure enough before dawn came messengers speeding to the forest hideouts.

'My lord Ingawa,' they said breathlessly. 'Many horsemen are coming from the West.'

'How many?' asked Ingawa.

'Oh, many, many.'

Ingawa called to Maghra: 'Go with this one and return to tell me how many Tauran warriors we must kill today.'

The faithful retainer took one of the Tauran horses seized in the marketplace, heaved up the young man behind him and sped away in a shower of grass and dirt.

Long before full light they were back. Maghra's face was grave. 'A full hundred, lord. In battle array.'

Ingawa looked round him at the awestruck townsfolk and laughed. 'That is one Tauran apiece for us, men, women and children.'

All laughed and then cheered.

The first Tauran warriors approached the town slowly. But when they saw the place was quiet they came in more boldly, six abreast, their officers riding carelessly ahead. They were here for revenge and amusement. When they saw the women setting up market stalls, they laughed and rode into the square. To their amazement, the women did not seem to notice them.

But when the square was half full of soldiers, the women suddenly threw off their hoods, picked up bows from the ground. A storm of arrows struck the first ranks.

As they turned about, doors opened in houses round the square. Volleys of arrows flew from all sides. Warriors fell mortally wounded, crashed into each other. They turned to flee. But at their back came a force of mounted lancers.

Surrounded and demoralized they fell like flies. By noon the battle was over. The remnants of the Tauran force were in full flight.

That evening as the townsfolk danced around great bonfires feasting and singing, someone came to Ingawa, in the forest camp.

'There is a priest who would speak with you, lord.'

Ingawa saw a tall man in monk's robes. His hood was back. The face was gentle, his hair long and fair. He held something behind his back. Then he spoke.

'You are Ingawa?'

'Yes.'

'I am Clarus the Hermit. I am bidden by the powers to give you this. You are the one to bear it.'

He held up a sword in its scabbard. Ingawa knew what it was.

'Exordo!' he gasped.

Home Sweet Home
Bayfield

5th November

Hi, yet again, friend.

I'm writing this at the end of our Bonfire Night party. Yes, we had one, in our small garden. Actually there was no bonfire, but fireworks, most of which went off over next door's air space. My brother did the honours; amazing, isn't it, him doing something for the rest of humanity? But this has been a very strange week.

It began with a disaster. The worst thing about holidays is coming back. On the first day at school, after half term, I walked into it up to my eyelashes.

I was on my own, no friends, no witnesses, no Blossom. How it happened I'll never know, but suddenly there was Oldfield, all teeth and hair, like something out at the full moon. I was in a corner with no way out.

'I've been looking for you, you little poof,' he said, 'and now I've found you.' I don't know who writes his scripts.

He picked me up — one-handed. All the blood drained down to my socks. I must have said something like, 'I don't know what you're talking about,' because he was hitting me and saying, 'Yes — you — do — you — little —'

All my past life was flashing before my eyes when someone spoke from behind this big lump of muscle and bone.

'Knock it off, Oldie.'

He put me down and turned round to destroy whoever was talking. It was Lance, my brother. Oldie was so shocked at being interrupted he said, stupidly: 'What's it got to do with you?'

'It's our kid,' said my brother. 'Just leave him. He's all right.' Me!

Then it got more bizarre. 'Come on, our kid,' he said, and walked me away with his arm round my shoulder. It made me feel weak at the knees. Then he said quietly: 'Listen, stay away from Clarrie. That's an order.' Then he punched me on the shoulder and walked away.

Something even more baffling happened when I got home. My mother asked if I'd like to have some friends round on Bonfire Night. I must have looked gobsmacked because she laughed. 'It's your brother's idea.'

So, this evening, they all came round, Soccer and Rat and Blossom. My mother laid on tea and talked a lot, mostly to Blossom. Soccer was dumbstruck and Rat doesn't understand polite conversation.

'Oh, your name's Curtiss, is it?' my mother asked Blossom. 'I think I've met your father, Richard Curtiss.'

She went ever so slightly pink. It's not often my mother does that. 'He and I crossed swords at the opting-out meeting.' She actually giggled. 'He was rather sarcastic about our side.'

Blossom groaned and looked down at the table. Mother went on:

'Oh, it was all very well argued. He knows his onions, does your father. And anyway, we won the vote.'

After the fireworks, Rat and Soccer went off and I showed Blossom my room. We sat and finished up the roast chestnuts and she said:

'Your brother's really quite nice...'

'For some reason he's being very nice,' I answered. I told her about being rescued from Oldie.

She grinned. 'I think I can explain. He and Oldie and a few more in the sixth fancy Helen Morten.'

'You mean the long blonde girl?'

'Uh huh.'

'So?'

'So, she's my sister, well, my stepsister.' Blossom made a face. 'I can see your jaw drop. I'm the ugly sister, it's the wrong way round. But she's OK, I like her, though she is totally disorganized, like my father. We don't have... I mean, my mother... died, three years ago. Where the two of them would be without me I don't know.'

Light was dawning. 'So that was why Oldie backed off when you told him... And that's why my brother started being human?'

We both started to laugh. I felt so good I did something very rash. I got out my writing, all the stuff on red paper and even my Sylvania stories on the blue paper, and showed her.

She read it all without a word, then she looked up and said: 'You wish your father was here, don't you, like I miss my mother now and then?'

That was weird, since I'd never seen my father. I suppose really it was more that I just wished he was alive.

My brother did the boy-scout bit and saw Blossom home. As she got her coat on she winked at me as if to say: 'This way he gets to see Helen.'

When he got back he was in a very good mood. We chatted a bit about school, exams, etc. He was so friendly, I was nearly tempted into doing something else rash. I nearly spoke to him about that airmail letter I'd seen in the hall.

But I didn't. I still don't trust my brother. Not after what he said about Keith Clarridge.

SYLVANIA QUEST

Gaw Penhallon

Chapter Eight
Ingawa's Oath

Clarus the priest solemnly held up the sword still in its sheath. Ingawa touched it with mingled feelings of awe and triumph.

As his fingers rested on the hilt a great rush of power flowed through his body. But as he moved to take hold of the sword, Clarus placed a restraining hand on his arm.

Looking around cautiously to make sure that the two of them were not overheard, the young priest said: 'Before you draw this blade, O Ingawa, you must make a solemn promise.'

'What is that?' asked Ingawa whose fingers itched to flourish the magic blade.

Clarus gave him a deep look, then answered: 'When you draw Exordo you will be disappointed because it seems just like an ordinary sword, no runes, no inscriptions, no bright gleam.

'That is its power. No one will know that you possess it, thus no one will seek to steal it from you. The power is in the holder who must prove himself truly worthy of it.'

'How, how?' uttered Ingawa eagerly.

'First by being loyal to the people of Sylvania and their queen. Second by never boasting of the mighty invincible power that you possess. I know that the first promise is easy. But the second is not. In some moment of crisis, to rally your followers you may reveal the secret.'

'Never, never,' swore Ingawa fervently.

'Do not speak too soon,' said Clarus. 'If you do break this promise the sword will vanish from your grasp. No power can prevent this. It will return to my charge only to be yielded up when a new champion arises.'

A great light dawned on Ingawa. He said: 'So that is why great Anedar lost the sword. Because he spoke of it. I shall never do this. My lips are sealed, O Clarus.'

'Remember, if you break your oath, all is lost.'

'Tell me, Clarus,' said Ingawa, 'were you not afraid to hold the sword? Men would do anything to take it.'

The priest smiled. 'I am beyond fear of men's violence. The sword can leave me only when the Powers tell me to hand it over, or when I am dead. You are the chosen one.'

'Why not my brother Tancelo, a mightier warrior than me?' stammered Ingawa.

Clarus shook his head. 'I may not reveal to you the reasons why you are chosen and not he. I may not reveal to you where your brother is or what he does. That you will know in good time. Now I shall hand you the sword. Do you swear to be true?'

'I swear.'

'Then take the sword of Exordo, O Ingawa, saviour of Sylvania.'

With these fateful words, the priest disappeared into the forest.

English
Update Letter to
Pen Friend

The High School
Bayfield, Oxon.

28th November

Hi.

It is some time since I last wrote you about my new school. It is new no longer. I have been here at Bayfield High for nearly three months. In fact, though no one will say this officially, everyone has begun the countdown to the Christmas holidays.

Meanwhile some are heavily involved in sports events, which I will not dwell on. Though I must mention the gruelling cross-country run last week in which *everyone* was heavily involved, particularly in the mud which abounds in the countryside at this time of year.

And, of course, some are heavily involved in activities like the school concert or play. Ear-splitting noises can be heard emitting from the music department, as budding musicians try for the umpteenth (or should that be oompahteenth?) time to get a simple tune right. I am fortunately tone-deaf and take no part in such proceedings.

Agonized cries can be heard from the Drama Department, where most of the drama comes from the teacher's efforts to get the play ready for the big night.

To my surprise, I have been asked to prepare some of my letters to a pen friend, for a display on Open Day.

Open Day, of course, is when your parents come to school to see how their offspring are progressing. This is an occasion for some trepidation, as well as perhaps a little amusement.

For the first time you see what sort of parents your friends have. For the first time you begin to understand what makes them tick.

And you get a chance to see your own parents in a new light as they talk to your teacher. It is not always agreeable to have two other people discuss you as if you were not there.

But, do not despair. Even if the general verdict of both school and home is that you are a disaster area, life will still go on and it is only four weeks to Christmas.

Yours,

Wain

22, Croxton Avenue
Bayfield

6th December

Hi, for real this time.

Parents' Evening began badly, but got better. As I came into the hall with my mother, who should be on door duty but Keith Clarridge. He gave me a grin and said: 'Hi, Wain, long time no see.'

I just went hot and cold and mumbled something. The fact is that since my brother told me to stay away from Keith, I have done. I don't know why I should do what my brother says, but I have done. It's rotten in a way, but I couldn't help it.

The place was crowded with parents and people. It was so riveting that I'm afraid I forgot about Keith by the end of the evening.

Soccer was there with his dad who is about twice as big as his son. Imagine that. I could hear him talking away across the hall, to Mr Sandeman, while we were waiting for our turn.

Soccer's dad said: 'I always tell Graham (at first I didn't know who he meant) he's got to put his back into his school work. It's not enough to be good at sports.'

I had to smile a bit at the idea of Soccer being good at anything, but then I thought maybe he was lucky having a dad who thought the world of him.

But it makes you realize how little parents know about *us*.

Rat's mother and father were there. I could see he was trying to keep them away from us. And no wonder. They were arm in arm. And all that garbage he gave us about them not talking to each other. People are amazing.

But wait till I tell you the most amazing thing. Who should walk in but Blossom and her father, Mr Richard Curtiss, otherwise known as – Kent Farrell!

It came on me in a blinding flash. I remembered when Kent Farrell came on his school visit and Blossom was so embarrassed because he was talking about 'observing closely the people around you'.

When all the teacher-parent business was over she brought him across to us. He remembered me (!) and said something about 'How's the writing?'

But, if I am honest, I'll admit he paid more attention to my mother. There was quite a bit of chat while Blossom smirked, yes, actually smirked at me.

In the end we all got into Kent's car (I can't and won't think of him as Mr Curtiss) and drove to their place for supper. It was one of these tall houses, with a green front door and green shutters to the windows.

After a bite to eat which Kent laid on in the kitchen, my mother and he went off for a drink in another room.

Blossom and I retired upstairs to her room which is about twice as big as mine and twice as untidy. All this stuff about having to look after her father and stepsister because they don't know what day it is!

We played Scrabble. She won. I can think of lots of long words, but she is much better at adding bits to my brilliant inventions, and getting rid of all her letters while I am working out what to put down next.

She pointed to the board and said: 'That's your trouble, Wain. You don't fit things together. I thought everybody knew Kent Farrell was my father.'

'Well, why didn't you tell me?' I was narked.

'Because I didn't want to embarrass you, stupid.'

There was a noise downstairs, the front door going. She put a finger to her lips and we sidled to the door. My brother and her stepsister Helen were in the hall carrying loads of textbooks.

'Ha, ha,' whispered Blossom. 'I expect they'll tell Dad they've been in the library. Revising, that's the new name for it.'

Then she pulled me back into her room while the two of them went up the stairs.

'Helen's got the whole top floor as a flat. She's jammy.'

'Jammy?' I asked.

'Oh, that's one of Father's Lancashire expressions. It means lucky.'

She giggled: 'It's self-contained and there's a staircase outside, like a fire escape. She can come and go without anybody else knowing. No wonder half the sixth form Romeos want to keep in with her.'

'Get off,' I said.

'Oh, she doesn't really use that staircase. She always comes through the house. Our father might be a bit disorganized, but he's rather old-fashioned and strict in his way.'

'What I can't understand,' I told Blossom, 'is what your sister sees in my brother. I mean she's got everything, looks and brains. He's, well, a thug and thick as two planks.'

She stared at me. 'Oh, it's like that between you, is it, Wain? Maybe they're like the magnets, you know, like poles repel, unlike poles attract.'

'But, I mean. He's mad on going in the Army. What does she think about that?'

Blossom shook her head. 'I don't think she likes it. She went to Greenham Common when she was sixteen. Maybe she's going to reform him.'

'Waste of time. Once he's finished with college, if he gets in, he'll join up, and become a general, if he doesn't — get killed or something.'

Blossom came across and squeezed my shoulder. 'Let's change the subject a bit. Tonight, history's being made.'

'History?'

'Yes. All of both our families are under one roof. That's something, isn't it?'

When she said that I remembered the dream I had about living in Kent Farrell's house. I almost told Blossom about it. But then I didn't because suddenly I remembered that airmail letter on the mat at home, and I knew then, for certain, it was from Argentina.

English Essay   The High School
<u>A Football Fiasco</u>   Bayfield, Oxon.

                                10th December

Nothing happens at the weekend we always complain, when asked to write about it. Life at home, so it seems, is one endless boring round of meals, chores (if not avoidable), homework and television, hardly anything worth remembering.

But this Sunday was different.

My friend Graham, whom I go jogging with when I can struggle up in the mornings, invited me to a soccer match.

Not to play, of course. Indeed I would not mention such a game, out of loyalty to the school where rugby is the official brand of mayhem.

But this was the weekend and I was off duty. And in any case he knew better than invite me to be a member of the team. I was there as a spectator. The day on which I willingly take part in anything more violent than Scrabble, has yet to dawn.

I went along to oblige my friend, but also, I must confess, out of a certain curiosity. He was playing in the Bayfield Junior League, and he assured me that this would be a 'needle' match. This means apparently that the two teams cannot wait to destroy each other.

In fact, most of the time, it was a clean match, with both teams playing hard – rather boring, in fact. My friend Graham made one or two rather good saves, including one over the bar which he swears almost took his fingernails off.

The other brilliant save came in the closing moments of the match, when the score was two all. The crowd, apart from myself and a dog who wandered on to the pitch now and then, was entirely made up of the parents of the boys in both teams.

They became very excited from time to time, mostly when they thought their offspring were being hard done by, and quite frenzied when the opposing team made a last-minute rush for a deciding goal.

Their striker struck, but my friend Graham stopped the ball. Well, the ball caught him full in the stomach and though tears came to his eyes, he held on to it. I felt the pain more than he did.

The crowd roared, half with joy, half with fury, then fell to violently disputing whether Graham was over the line or not. The referee (and half the crowd) said no, the other half said yes.

The referee declared the match over and sent the players off the pitch which made room for the crowd who poured on – all forty-four of them (I suppose there were two parents per player but one never knows). My friend's father, who is Chairman of the League, tried to restore order, but the parent who was trainer of the other side offered to give him a 'bunch of fives' whatever that may be.

The police were finally called and a good time was had by all.

SYLVANIA QUEST

Gaw Penhallon

Chapter Nine
Tancelo's Return

After Clarus had gone, Ingawa went to his bed and slept
with the sword Exordo at his side. His own blade, which
he had brought from the citadel, he put carefully back
into his bundle. It had served him well and he would keep
it as a reminder.

When dawn came he called a council of war – Maghra,
Rodon, the girl Blodwen and some of the boldest young
people from the town. There it was decided that some
should stay behind to defend the town. The rest, as many
as had horses and weapons captured in the battle, to the
number of forty, were formed into a troop of cavalry.

Maghra aided by Blodwen, who had a strange authority with the youth, spent some days teaching them the art of war. Then he told Ingawa:

'If they are not now ready they will never be ready. With this troop we may harass small bands of Taurans and hope to beat them.'

But to the amazement of the others, Ingawa shook his head. 'No, we shall not fight that way. We shall raise an army and defeat the Taurans in pitched battle, so that all may know that their doom is near.'

Maghra shook his head. The others stood and stared. But Blodwen clapped her hands and cried: 'Yes, yes.'

So Ingawa sent Rodon to roam around the villages and pass the word that Prince Ingawa, son of Anedar, called all true Sylvanians to arms. Those who could bring a Tauran's arms and horse would be welcome in Ingawa's army. How they obtained them was their own business.

Then Ingawa, with his band, returned to the foot of Mount Rosaron and waited. Soon hundreds, armed and mounted, joined them. The work of training began. But the enemy was not idle and soon came news that a Tauran army was on the march. The time had come.

While the Tauran troops were still marching through the passes, in the fond belief that they were going to crush a peasant rabble, Ingawa's forces attacked them by surprise from all points of the compass.

So unexpected and ferocious was the attack that the Taurans were demoralized. They tried to flee but were cut down without mercy.

Before the year ended Ingawa's armies had won three battles and as the first winter snow began to fall, they camped in the plain before the citadel.

With a few companions, Ingawa rode across the famous bridge and entered the fortress. No one challenged them. Steps and passages were empty, echoing.

In the throne room sat Queen Sylva in her majesty. 'Welcome my son,' she said, but her voice was quiet.

She was not alone. At her side stood Tancelo in full armour, and next to him, bearded and brutal, the tyrant Tauro.

Bleak House
Bayfield

18th December

From your glum friend.

You may well goggle or boggle. Is this the cheerful chap who was having a giggle at the expense of those good sports, the parents of Bayfield Junior League, only last week?

The fact is I am choked, worse still I am depressed, so much that I don't even want to joke about it. Just when it seemed, for once in the history of the universe, that life was going my way, things have started to come to pieces.

Number One. I have just had a row with Blossom. Well, a non-row, which is worse. I am not speaking to her. She knows why and she is not speaking to me. Which makes two of us.

And it is not just a spat between friends, it is more serious than that, it is a betrayal of trust.

Number Two is that what has happened turns out to be in my brother's favour. He gets what he wants, I don't. I just get let down.

What am I rambling on about? Be patient. I will let the tale unfold exactly as it folded itself.

Kent Farrell, I mean Richard Curtiss, came round last night again. Nothing strange in that. Recent weeks have seen much toing and froing between our hovel in Croxton Avenue and that tall house with green thingies in Milbourne Terrace. Blossom and me having Scrabble sessions, my brother and her stepsister having 'study' sessions, ha ha.

And our parents doing their own toing and froing. Long, quiet talking sessions, beyond the reach of eavesdroppers, worse luck. But this evening was different... I could tell by the way Kent looked when he came in and the speed with which I was ushered out of the lounge where I had been very comfortable doing my homework in front of the small screen.

Offspring have an instinct about the behaviour of parents and in my family where information is at its minimum, instinct is my main asset.

I lingered in the hall and since the door was not quite closed I could hear most of the discreet conversation in which the word 'they' played a very important part. They being Helen and my brother.

It seems 'they' are rapidly becoming 'serious' and would like to move in together. For one ghastly moment I thought Kent was going to say 'Your son must make an honest woman of my daughter' or 'Are his intentions honourable?'

But it wasn't like that. It was sort of humdrum talk about exams, college, etc., or what about my brother's plans to conquer the world, or get himself posted to Pitcairn Island or somewhere?

It was, to be honest, getting a bit boring. They were going into such detail about things of no interest, when I heard that 'they' would be moving into Milbourne Terrace, where Kent Farrell would be on hand, day and night, slaving over his hot word processor. But 'they' would have to wait till they were eighteen.

At this point I did some rapid calculations. I had to endure my brother under the same roof for only three months, two weeks and five days longer. I would only see him when I went over for Scrabble, and perhaps not even then.

Just as a wave of bliss overcame me, I heard my mother say: 'Richard, would you like a drink? While we're talking family matters, there is something you may...

like to know. Let us go and sit over by the window. It's more comfortable.'

Yes, and further from the door. I moved closer but their voices were lower. So I wandered upstairs and finished my homework, then listened to the radio. Mother does not allow TV in one's room, it's not good for one and we can't afford it — there's always a good reason why things cost too much.

I was listening to a quiz programme (all the contestants were complete plonkers) when there was a knock at the door. I sprang to it and Kent Farrell came in, envelope in hand, looking embarrassed.

'Hi, Kent,' I said to put him at his ease. He grinned and answered: 'Hi, Gaw, what's the word from Sylvania?'

I told him and he listened, but I knew he was not here to talk creative writing with me. It had to do with that envelope which eventually he handed me. It wasn't sealed. And inside was — another of my bits of red paper.

'You remember when you sent your Sylvania stories to me and other papers got mixed up with them. I returned them.'

I nodded, my brain whizzing round. There was something not right about this.

'That sheet must have been left out. I knew you'd want it back and I wanted to apologize.'

106

'That's OK,' I said slowly, my eye running down the paper. The last sentence stood out. Someone had put a pencil exclamation mark by it. '… That night I dreamt we moved and lived in the same house as Kent Farrell.'

He guessed what I was reading. He said quietly: 'Nice thought, Wain. I'm very flattered,'… then very slowly: 'I wish life was as straightforward as dreams, don't you? But it isn't.'

He went out then. As I heard the front door close, two thoughts struck me like kicks in the teeth.

One: my brother would get to live in that house with green shutters, but I wasn't going to.

And Two, even worse: the red sheet in my hand had a later date on it than the other ones Kent had sent back to me. How had he got hold of this one? Who put the pencil mark on it? No prizes.

I'd trusted Blossom to look at my stories on Bonfire Night. She'd seen the red paper and sneaked it out, to show her father, behind my back.

SYLVANIA QUEST

Gaw Penhallon

Chapter Ten
Tauro's Plan

Ingawa's eyes swept the throne room. Apart from a handful of warriors no one else was present. He laughed.

'So, Tauro, you are here to surrender?'

The tyrant's face wore a terrible smile.

'You have a sense of humour, little Ingawa. No, I am not here to surrender, although my forces have suffered some trifling reverses.'

'Trifling?' cried Blodwen, at Ingawa's side. 'Our arms have utterly defeated your armies. Your time of conquest is over, Tauro.'

The tyrant shook his head. 'Not so. But the time of war is over and I have come to make peace. Let the noble Tancelo explain.'

'Since when did a prince of Sylvania speak for Tauran scum?' demanded Ingawa in fury.

'Little brother,' said Tancelo condescendingly, 'I am speaking to show you that this generous offer of peace is real. It is made with my full approval.'

'So for this past year, you have not been seeking the magic sword, but skulking in Tauro's court which Sylvania's sons and daughters have battled?'

Tancelo's face was red with rage. Then he said: 'The magic sword is nowhere to be found. It is gone.'

Ingawa longed to draw the sword at his belt and flourish it in his brother's face, but he managed to control himself.

'Very well,' he said, 'tell me what terms Tauro offers that we should grant him peace?'

Tancelo looked at Queen Sylva then spoke.

'The Tauran army will leave Sylvanian soil. Our two countries will be united in everlasting peace.'

'What is the guarantee?'

'The marriage of King Tauro and Queen Sylva in this very palace.'

Ingawa burst into bitter laughter.

'Mother, do you allow your son to mock you?'

Queen Sylva did not look at Ingawa. She said: 'I have accepted this offer so that his hopeless war may end.'

'Mother, it is not hopeless. My army camps at your gate. Before winter is over, we shall drive the last Tauran from our soil.'

Tauro laughed. 'Little Ingawa. For every Tauran soldier in Sylvania, ten wait outside. You cannot defeat us.'

'Tauro,' said Ingawa, 'either you withdraw from Sylvania, or I will hang you from these battlements.'

Queen Sylva turned pale, but Tauro laughed again.

'A man after my own heart. Hang me if you wish. But the moment my escort, hidden across the river, learns this, my armies will burn and kill their way across your realm, inch by inch. Nothing will be left.'

Sylva rose. 'Ingawa, accept! You have no choice.'

Against his will Ingawa shouted: 'We shall triumph. Know this. The sword at my belt is Exordo. The priest Clarus gave it me. With it our forces are invincible.'

Tauro laughed for a third time.

'Which sword, little man? There is no sword at your belt.'

Ingawa looked down. The magic sword had vanished.

English
Pen Friend Update

The High School
Bayfield, Oxon.

19th December

Hi, it's Wain, again.

We are *almost* there. One last push and we reach the end of term, the goal we have been aiming for since we started the new school.

Everyone and everything has now settled down, or should have done. The awkward subjects, the awkward teachers, all have been sorted out in the mind and entered in the inner computer, so to speak. Now we know, without thinking even, who to avoid, what to expect.

The school, classrooms, labs, corridors, cloakrooms, hall, gym, playing fields, playground, bike sheds, that all seemed so big, so forbidding and strange when term began, are now so familiar you feel you have been here all your life, well almost.

There have been some difficult moments, perhaps some dangerous ones, even, certainly some tricky situations, but you have learnt how to cope, how to get by and even how to joke about it all; laugh, clown, laugh. Seriously though, school can be quite funny sometimes.

Most important of all, you have made at least one friend.

Maybe you even have a gang, possibly you are in a mob and have achieved maximum security. But best of all there are one or two friends with whom you are completely at ease, dare one say, people you can really trust.

But here a note of caution. Supposing you find that the person you trusted most, isn't trustworthy? Supposing you find the one you confided in does not respect your confidence?

What is the point in sharing secrets if they are not kept but immediately passed on to someone else, plunging you into embarrassment or worse?

Funnily enough, this is supposed to be the age of communication but in fact there is a lot of non-communication going on as well. Adults do not tell young people things they ought to know. You are left to guess what is happening, even in one's own home and family.

When there is this gap between parents, say, and offspring, then friends become even more vital to your peace of mind.

And if friends are not to be counted on then who can?

22, Croxton Avenue
Bayfield, Oxon.

New Year's Eve

Are you there?

It's nearly midnight. No, the folk at No. 22 Croxton have not been celebrating, far from it. I am seeing the New Year in on my own, in my own room I mean, looking out at the snow. The whole world's turned white.

I'd better do this like a diary to make sure I have remembered everything, to try and get it straight in my mind.

December 23rd: Up early, not to go jogging. Too cold. But I heard voices in the hall, raised voices which does not happen often in our home.

I peered sleepily over the banister rail to see my mother and my brother having a wrestling match in the hall. No, rather a tug-of-war over who was going to have an envelope which must have come in the post. Mother was shouting, quietly.

'Lance. Just let go.'

Her face was pink. Lance was pale, strange for him. His eyes looked black. 'I want to know!' he was saying. It was weird, as though he were going to burst out crying.

Then Mother looked up and saw me. She turned pale. Lance looked up. She snatched the letter, marched out of the hall. He followed like a shot. Now the voices were very quiet. I did not sneak down and earwig. No way.

But I knew, I knew what it was all about. My guess about that first airmail letter was right. Bang on target. My father *is* alive and he's in touch with my mother.

I didn't have long to brood, because Mother came upstairs and said I should get my 'kit' together. She still uses words like that. Later in the afternoon I was packed off to Grandmother's, and glad to go.

Christmas Eve: I helped Grandmother put up decorations, nothing much, just one or two bits in each room. Then we had mince pies in the kitchen. Grandfather was out at the golf club.

'Is he playing golf in this weather?' I asked. She smiled, well she grinned, and said: 'Your grandfather does not play golf. He just likes to spend his time in the company of men like himself.'

Then she amazed me. She looked over the table and said: 'You'll be like him when you grow up. In looks. He's small like you. He married a girl who was a head taller than him, and we had a son who grew bigger than both of us. Then he married a tall woman and had a big son. Until you came along, your grandfather was the only titch in the family.

'Your grandfather joined up as a boy in the band. He had no parents. The Army was mother and father to him. He had high hopes of your father.'

'Gran,' I said, 'my father...'

But she put a finger to her lips. Grandfather was letting himself in by the front door.

Christmas Day: Grandfather amazed me by giving me a book as a present, a thesaurus, a sort of super dictionary, with all different words that mean the same thing.

'Help you with your writing,' he said, then out he went. Grandmother smiled. I guessed she'd put him up to it. He came back for dinner. Nobody said much and he dozed off afterwards.

It was fresh and frosty outside, so Grandmother and I went walking with Winston. We talked a lot. I mean, she talked and I listened.

'Gawain,' she said, 'it's hard having a parent who wants you to go far when there isn't very far to go.

You're good at Geography, so you'll understand. In 1947 when your father was born, the Army came home from India. When he was going to school we were pulling out of the Middle East. When he joined the Army we were pulling out of Africa. Our world has grown smaller.'

We stopped to wait for Winston who was making a huge effort to cock his leg. Grandmother talked counting on her fingers.

'Where can the Army go now, apart from Northern Ireland, or odd-jobbing for the United Nations? The Falklands, Gibraltar, Hong Kong, Bermuda, South Georgia, Cayman Islands, Pitcairn...' She laughed. 'An ape sanctuary, a seal sanctuary, a floating stock exchange, four tax havens and a couple of weather stations. No glory.

'When your father was posted missing in Argentina, it seemed right for his father. The last great venture worth risking a soldier's life.'

Winston caught up with us. We went on, the ground crackling under our feet.

'I wouldn't talk like this to your brother. He's set on the Army. Wants to do great things, like his father.'

I stopped Grandmother. 'My father. He's alive.'

She nodded.

'In Argentina?'

She nodded again. 'In a remote mountain village.' She took my arm. 'Your mother always hoped he had survived. Even if he'd gone over to the other side. A dead hero's not much of a husband.'

I burst out: 'Lance would rather have him dead.'

'Gawain,' she said gently, 'Lance wants him as he was — unchanged. We all — want things to be as we'd like them. And now your father's in touch, your mother's not sure what it means, for her, for you…'

Suddenly I remembered Kent Farrell's words — if only life was as straightforward as dreams. Having my father alive was one thing. Having him back was another.

Boxing Day: Grandmother said: 'You haven't had a present from me yet.' She took me up into the attic stacked with all kinds of junk and pulled out an old suitcase.

'I kept this for you. Lance wouldn't — want it. He wouldn't know what to do with it. You will.'

It was full of books with worn bindings.

'When your father was your age, he was the despair of Grandfather. Head in a book. That was when we were stationed in Guyana. Then, when we were posted away, he changed: no more books; instead — sport, training. Your grandfather was happy. But I kept these in case someone needed them. I think you do, Gawain.'

December 27th: As I came home on the train it started to snow.

The books are still in their case. I don't feel like looking at them, yet.

English Homework   The High School
A Winter's Day   Bayfield, Oxon.

5th January

Snow began to fall last week, while we were still on holiday. Perhaps some people hoped it would go on snowing and block the roads to school so that even the most heroic (insane) pupils could not plough their way through.

It was not to be. Just after New Year's Day the snow began to thaw. It seemed that it would melt and run away. But no, before that happened, came a Great Freeze.

Pavements and gardens were coated with a hard white crust like an iced cake, while salt trucks and traffic cleared the roads.

Fields and parks lay blank under a pale winter sun, only marked by the footprints of a solitary dog wandering from tree to tree, or a jogger bent on carrying out a New Year resolution regardless of the consequences.

At school for once the playing fields, so often the scene of mud-spattered massacre, stretched still and white, the goal posts barely visible against the shining background.

Those who venture out of the classrooms for a solitary walk (the playing fields and snowball fighting are under a strict ban) find a world of silence where the ground slopes down to the pond, frozen hard among its circle of bare, black trees.

The ice seems thick enough to walk on and there is much classroom talk about how thick it might be. No doubt before it melts some bold spirit will brave the frown of the authorities and run across its creaking expanse.

But now, like the fields above, it stretches level and clear, concealing what lies beneath. Winter holds its secrets only to be revealed when the weather changes.

It is like looking into the future. One can only guess and wonder at what one may discover tomorrow.

SYLVANIA QUEST

Gaw Penhallon

Chapter Eleven
Ingawa Goes Alone

Sadly Ingawa left his band across the bridge, leaving the citadel behind. Silently they rode back into their camp. The waiting cohorts looked at their downcast faces in total bewilderment.

Ingawa called a council. The tent was crowded with the young but battle-hardened commanders. Next to him stood Blodwen, Maghra and Rodon, the faithful three.

'Brothers, sisters,' said the Prince. 'The fighting is over. We must accept the peace offered by Tauro. He will marry our Queen Sylva and his armies will leave Sylvania.'

'What does this mean, Lord Ingawa?' asked one of the commanders who only six months before had been a simple goatherd in the Sylvanian mountains. 'We had beaten them. Why should we accept this shame?'

'Because Tauro's armies outnumber us by ten to one. We cannot defeat him.'

'But we defeated armies many times our size before,' said another commander.

Ingawa shook his head. 'We won because Clarus gave me the magic sword Exordo. And because I broke my promise and boasted of it, I have lost the sword. I cannot lead you now.'

'What shall we do, Lord Ingawa?' they asked.

'Accept the peace,' he answered sadly. 'Go back to your farms, and your families, live your lives as before.'

The council members started to leave the tent, but Blodwen spoke heatedly.

'I remember when Clarus came to you, Ingawa. That was *after* our first battle. We can fight without magic swords. I for one will not accept this peace. Those who agree with me shall follow where I lead.'

With that she turned her back on Ingawa and marched out. Half a dozen commanders followed her. But most obeyed Ingawa and ordered their men to go home. Ingawa was left with Maghra and Rodon.

'What will you do now, lord?' asked Maghra.

Ingawa sighed. 'I shall go and beg Clarus' pardon. Maybe he will relent when he hears how the oath was broken. Do not come with me. I shall go alone.'

Next day the army rode away from the citadel. Blodwen and her followers had gone already in the night. Alone Ingawa set out.

On his back he carried his old bundle. He gave armour and horse to Maghra who bade him farewell, sadly. Then Ingawa marched away into the forests where the trees were black against the snow. He marched week after week.

Everywhere he sought Clarus the priest. Sometimes the trail was cold, sometimes warm. Clarus was near. Or Clarus had just gone before him.

At last when winter was nearly over and snows started to thaw, he found a hut by a frozen mountain lake and sat down to rest. He heard his name called and, raising his weary head, saw Clarus, gaunt and thin in his long robe.

He knelt before the priest and pleaded, but Clarus said: 'The sword stays hidden till another shall come who can keep the promise. Only I know where it lies.'

'Then you shall tell us, priest.'

The voice came from behind them. Turning they saw Tauro the tyrant, hand on hips, and a little way off Tancelo.

22, Croxton Avenue
Bayfield, Oxon.

6th January

Hi, at last.

I say, at last, because it is really some time since I faxed you. In fact all this was written down after I came home from hospital later on. But I've put the date when it happened to keep things in order in my mind, which, to be honest, is still a bit confused.

Why I walked past the computer block that afternoon when school was over, I do not know. I was on my own. But I had no reason to go in there.

But the funny thing is, when I look back, I wonder whether I didn't do it on purpose. Some people must have thought I did. Anyway, this is what happened.

It was getting dark — well, the sky was grey and low. And it was freezing cold. As I trudged along, I heard someone call 'Wain!'

It was Keith Clarridge. I didn't turn round, but I slowed down and he caught up with me. His voice sounded jokey and serious.

'How's it going, Wain? What's the word from Sylvania?'

I mumbled something. I heard him sort of sigh, then he said:

'Are you in a hurry, Wain? I wanted a word.'

I suppose I wanted to clear off. And yet I wanted to talk to him.

We walked on to the edge of the playing fields and down towards the pond. The snow crunched under our feet. Then Keith said:

'I'm leaving school. My grandmother's ill. She's looked after me since I was tiny. Now I'm looking after her.'

'What about your A's?'

He shrugged. 'They can wait. Anyway I want to get away from this — stinking place.'

I said nothing. I think I know what he meant.

'Wain. I know your brother told you to stay away from me. I was a bit hurt when you stopped dropping in for a chat. But I didn't blame you.'

I wanted to say something, but the words were stuck fast in my throat. Keith carried on.

'I'm used to that sort of stupidity now. Worse things have been said about me, and worse things done. But I didn't want you to think that I was taking advantage. That I was – you know – after you.'

I stood still and stared at him. My mouth must have dropped open. He smiled as if I'd given him the right answer.

'We're friends, yes?' he said. 'Maybe we'll see one another now and then, for a chat?'

I still couldn't speak so he put his hand out. 'All the best, Wain.'

We shook hands. My fingers were still in his, when out of the corner of my eye I saw two figures hurrying along the gravel track. The snow cover had muffled their steps. But I saw my brother and Oldfield just before they were on top of us.

'Clarridge, I warned you,' barked my brother in his Sandhurst voice. 'I told you to leave my brother alone.'

Keith started to say something, but I spoke first. My voice sounded squeaky. 'Oh, leave it, Lance. You're out of order.'

My brother gaped. I'd never spoken to him like that, ever.

But Oldfield made an animal noise, lunged across me and hit Keith in the face. He fell backwards. I heard his head strike the ground. Blood shot up from his nose. Slowly he picked himself up, shaking, as if he were dazed. Oldfield went for him again, but my brother grabbed his arm.

'Cool it, Oldie. That's enough.'

While Oldie wrestled with my brother, Keith staggered off down the slope to the pond. Oldie pulled himself loose, ran after Keith who blundered into the fence above the frozen water. It must have been rotten. It gave way and he went crashing on to the ice, picked himself up again, wobbled out to the middle, then stood there, his face red and white in patches.

My brother dragged Oldie away. 'Leave him alone! Come on.' They ran up the slope. I heard them laugh as they disappeared in the gloom.

I called out: 'Come on, Keith. It's OK. They've gone.'

Slowly he started to come towards the bank, swaying as if he was drunk. I scrambled down the slope ready to help him up, when the ice gave an awful groan.

Then came a crack like a gun and Keith was sliding into the gap. I looked round and shouted. No, I screamed. 'Help, help!'

But no one came.

But now I was in a complete spin. I grabbed at the palings in the broken fence and a great chunk of it, maybe two metres, came away in my hands. Then I tobogganed down on to the ice, dragging it with me, and heaved it across the ice towards Keith.

Only half of him was out of the water. It was black and spreading over the ice. But his arm hooked over the broken wood that stuck out from the firm ice. I crawled nearer, shouting all the time. I can still hear my voice.

Then it all began to collapse under me and I felt the water sucking me down. My hand reached Keith's again. We were going down. I was passing out.

There was a high-pitched noise and shouting. I was being dragged away, my hand snatched from Keith's. I was lifted up, carried like a baby. My eyes opened. I looked up — into Ape's face!

'Where's Clarridge, sir?' I asked.

'Where you're going. In the ambulance.'

SYLVANIA QUEST

Gaw Penhallon

Chapter Twelve
The Death of Clarus

Tauro laughed at the astonishment on the faces of Clarus and Ingawa.

'Ha, little man. Your brother guessed that you might seek out the priest to beg him let you have the magic sword again.'

'Yes, brother,' added Tancelo. 'We came to urge you not to break the peace. Let the magic sword stay hidden. Give up this quest and let our land be free from bloodshed.'

'Fool,' roared Tauro, turning on Tancelo. 'Do you think you little brother will ever accept this peace? There will be no peace until the sword is found and in my hands, and I am master of Sylvania.'

Tancelo was aghast.

'But you gave me your word as a knight and a king that if you marry Sylva, then our lands would live in friendship.'

'Idiot,' swore Tauro. 'I only sought your help to persuade your mother. She would never have agreed otherwise.'

Tancelo's face was white with shame, but Tauro turned to Clarus. 'Priest, hand over the sword!'

'Never while I have breath in my body.'

'That is an easy matter to arrange,' roared the tyrant. With one blow of his mailed fist he sent the priest bloodstained to the ground. As Clarus tried to rise, Tauro drew his sword to deliver the fatal blow. Horrified, Tancelo tried to stop him, but the blade swung down.

Now Ingawa snatched from the bundle on his back the old trusted sword he had brought from the citadel and like lightening parried Tauro's blow. The blades clashed. Tauro growled horribly.

'Run, Clarus, run,' cried Ingawa and sprang once more between them. The priest fled stumbling away across the frozen pool. Tauro rushed after him, sword swinging in the air, bent on murder.

But as the priest reached the middle of the lake there came a creaking and a cracking sound. A long black line opened in the white surface of the ice. In that instant the figure of Clarus, arms held aloft, was seen to vanish from sight into the dark waters.

Cursing violently, Tauro returned to the shore. He glared for a moment at the two brothers then whistled shrilly. Out of the trees rode a dozen Tauran soldiers.

'Take the little man, and bind him. I want him to be at his mother's wedding. He can walk behind us. That will cool his lust for battle.'

As the cavalcade, with Ingawa dragged behind, set off, Tauro shouted: 'Wait. Where is Tancelo?'

But Ingawa's brother had vanished from the scene.

English   The High School

<u>A Stay in Hospital</u>   Bayfield, Oxon.

12th January

I was in hospital for four days, which was quite enough, thank you. In fact, this very big and very cheerful doctor told me there was nothing wrong with me and they wanted me out because they needed the bed for someone who was really ill. He was only joking, I think.

The first day I felt really sick and weak and sorry for myself. The second day I found it interesting because there were all sorts of tests – they thought there might be bugs in the pond water. I could have told them a thing or two about what is in that pond. But I liked all the toing and froing and finding out the names of the nurses and the staff nurse and ward manager and secretary, etc.

On the third day, I began to get a bit bored and count the minutes to the next meal or wander round to the shop or hang about the kitchen until they chased me out.

There was no one to talk to most of the time. My friend Keith was in the next bed but he was either asleep or they were talking about him behind the curtains. Sister tells me he had a lucky escape. I know.

The other people in the ward were mostly very old and didn't say much except at visiting time.

I felt sorry for the ones who had no visitors, except the vicar, and just stared out of the window.

First visitor through the door on Day One was my mother, bringing among other goodies, my writing kit... Then on Day Two, Mr Sandeman my form tutor and Mr Earnshaw the PE master kindly came in for a long chat. It was Mr Earnshaw who pulled me out of the pond.

On Day Three, my friends all came. They brought a box of chocolates for me, and surprise surprise, they noshed the lot themselves. Well, I had three.

On Day Four my mother came for me. My friend Keith was a lot better. His eyes were open and he was able to say goodbye to me.

Kent Farrell, that is Mr Curtiss, drove Mother and me home.

Home Sweet Home

12th January

Hi, he said weakly.

I've been back at school a day or two now but not quite got back to normal yet. I mean the things that happened are still going through my mind. I'll tell you, just to clear the head.

That first day in hospital was dire. I kept throwing up, with that filthy pond water and everything. I think that's why they kept me in, for tests to see if I'd got rabies or something.

I could hear them moving about round Keith in the next bed – nurses and doctors coming and going. Now and then, when it looked interesting enough for me to forget how I felt, they put the curtains round.

When I wasn't being sick and being kindly held up over

a basin, or whipped in a wheelchair down to the toilets (now that was weird), I was sleeping.

Once I woke to find my mother looking at me, saying something like 'How're you feeling, Bunny?' She hasn't called me that since I was totally tiny and it made me feel all weak and helpless. I thought it was a dream, but afterwards I found she'd left some chocolates and my writing case.

I had a bad moment when I wondered if she might have read some of my stuff but banished the thought. Mother does not do sneaky things like that.

After dozing all day I was kept awake all night by some old geezer who snored away like a herd of elephants. Every now and then the night nurse turned him round. Five minutes of blissful silence and I would nod off and he'd start again and wake me up.

I was totally amazed the next day when who should walk in but Sandy and Ape. They sat down on either side of my bed and smiled. Well, Sandy smiled and Ape sort of grimaced. They then began to grill me about WHAT HAPPENED AT THE POND?

What could I say? I was like that bloke in the courts — the one who was economical with the truth. I know what they mean when they say — the whole truth... Well, I told part.

I'd seen Keith in the middle of the pond. He'd tried to run across. I'd called to him and he'd turned back but the ice cracked and he went in.

What was he doing on the ice?... Why was the fence broken down? I couldn't say 'don't know', so I just rolled my eyes and looked blank.

What about the bruises on his face? I had an inspiration. He must have hit himself on the ice when he fell. Ape looked at me and raised his eyebrows.

'Clarridge had injuries on his face and the back of his head. He couldn't fall both ways. There is something more you can tell us, isn't there, Wain?'

His voice was so quiet and human, not his usual bullying roar, that I almost told him. But not quite. Sandy sort of signalled to Ape and they both got up.

'There we are,' said Sandy. When you get back to school you may remember things a bit more clearly. We think Clarridge was the victim of a brutal and cowardly attack and someone left him to drown. He was lucky you came along.'

It wasn't quite as bad as that, but it was close enough, and one of the someones was my brother. I played by the rules and said nothing more.

Next day Helen flowed in with flowers and a big 'get well' card for Keith. I got a kiss. Keith was asleep and she went. Later I sneaked over and tried to look at the signatures on the card. But Sister came and shooed me off to bed. When I next looked, the card had been put away somewhere, though the flowers were still in a vase on the table.

Then just as I was having a well-earned nap after lunch I heard this noise, people saying, 'Look at him' and giggling. I was awake in a flash and saw Soccer, Rat and believe it or not, Blossom.

Soccer carried the chocolates. He looked at them so sadly as he handed he box over that I had to open it right away and before they left it was empty. Rat lent me his Walkman. I was as gobsmacked as if he'd donated an arm or a leg.

Blossom said very little. She didn't really look at me. I was narked because although I'd started the not-talking bit, it was her fault. Still I felt let down when they all went.

Ten minutes later, I was listening to a radio quiz hoping it would send me to sleep when someone nudged me. It was Blossom. She'd sneaked back. I tried to look cool and stern but she said:

'Are you still mad at me?'

I didn't answer, I wanted to but couldn't. She whispered:

'I'm truly sorry, Wain. I just wanted Dad to see what you'd written about… you know… us all living in the same house. I should have asked. What did you think?'

I took a deep breath, I'd done enough porky pie-ing today. I told the truth: 'I thought you were just fixing up my mother to look after your helpless father. I thought you were manipulating.'

She turned so red I almost felt sorry. Then she grinned. 'Right first off, Wain. But' — she chewed at her lip — 'but I wouldn't have done it if I hadn't liked you.'

I said something rotten. It just came out. 'You were wasting your time. My father's still alive. He might come back. There's no way my mother... will...'

I stopped. Now she was crying. She stuck her knuckles in her mouth, then said quietly: 'We're still friends, aren't we?'

I couldn't speak so I nodded and she turned and ran out.

Next day when my mother collected me, Kent Farrell was waiting outside with the car. She got into the back seat and told me to sit next to the driver. He asked me about Sylvania. As it happened I'd been writing a chapter or two in the hospital. Then he stopped talking and no more was said till we got home. Then it was 'goodbye'.

But in that silence in the car I'd made my mind up. I wanted to blow the whistle on my brother and I knew the way to do it.

English Essay: The High School
Own Choice   Bayfield, Oxon.
<u>The Right Thing?</u>

19th January

One of the most confusing choices facing a pupil in his or her first year at school is how to do the right thing. Most people find the right answer by rephrasing the question – how to get out of trouble?

Those in charge, the teachers, may say, well, if you do what is right, then you'll stay out of trouble, no problem. If only that were so.

When teachers say you will keep out of trouble, they mean you will keep out of trouble with *them*. But what is much more difficult is keeping out of trouble with your friends, or your enemies.

Say something has been stolen. And say your form tutor threatens dire punishment on all and sundry if it not returned. Sometimes it is returned in secret and everyone, except the one who has to return it, is happy.

But say they don't. And say you know who has done the stealing? Suppose it is your best friend? Do you tell teacher?

In one way this is the right thing. On the other hand the worst thing you can do is tell tales, snitch, grass, etc.

Everybody hates the telltale. Even the teachers despise the one who informs.

So the right thing to do might be to tell the person who has done the stealing to put it back, on the quiet. This may work if it is your friend. But suppose it is your enemy, and suppose he or she is bigger than you? Who is going to protect you?

If you tell lies to the teachers, your friends may protect you. But if you tell the truth about your enemy, will the powers-that-be protect you? Can they protect you?

These are the thoughts in the mind of someone who does not want to be a creep, but does know right from wrong, especially when what has been done is so awful that there can't be any doubt about it.

What do you do when a friend or someone like that has done something really rotten? Do you shop them? Do you blow the whistle?

There's a question not easy to answer.

SYLVANIA QUEST

Gaw Penhallon

Chapter Thirteen
A Royal Wedding

The great throne room of the citadel of Sylvania was awash with music and colourful decoration. Lords and ladies from the capitals of Sylvania and Taura jostled with one another.

In the courtyard below the great windows stood a gilded carriage ready to bear away the proud green-eyed Queen to the realm of her husband. Bishops in full regalia of the churches of both realms were grouped on either side of the throne awaiting the two monarchs.

Everywhere were smiles and laughter. Only two faces showed no sign of joy. Grania the majestic white-haired

Queen Mother stood stony-faced in the corner of the hall. Next to her, closely watched by two Tauran officers, was Prince Ingawa, his head lowered in utter despair.

He had made his bid to recover the sword Exordo but all that he had achieved was the death of Clarus the priest. His heart was full of shame. And now he was compelled to watch his mother marry the tyrant.

But even in his despair he eyed the two guards. He wondered if he might overpower them and escape. But there were other Taurans in the hall, enough to make it too difficult.

A great blast of trumpets proclaimed the entrance of Tauro, huge and dark in his opulent scarlet robes. He wore a smile of triumph. With the death of Clarus he guessed that no one could find the magic sword and he would be master of both realms.

But for the moment he kept his thoughts hidden. Let the Queen believe he meant peace. His plans were for conquest.

True, Tancelo knew his plot. But he was lost somewhere in the forests. And the young rebel prince knew. But the Queen would never believe her angry son. Tauro knew that the Queen hated her new husband but he did not care. Sylvania was the prize and soon it would be his.

Another fanfare and the doors were flung wide. The

green-eyed Queen in her shining robes entered surrounded by her ladies. Slowly she advanced until she stood at one side of the throne facing the Tauran monarch with his escort.

The chief bishop raised his hand for silence.

'Loyal subjects,' he intoned. 'We are gathered together to witness the holy marriage of our beauteous Queen and the noble monarch of Taura. Let us...'

But before he could utter another word someone called from the end of the hall.

'Wait, Bishop. Before the wedding, let a wandering minstrel pay his homage to his beloved Queen and her future husband.'

'Who speaks?' asked the bishop.

A tall commanding figure, cowled and robed, took the centre of the hall, harp in hand. His voice boomed.

'I am called Dearna.'

22, Croxton Avenue

Bayfield

19th January

Hi.

My last two Sylvania stories were really disguised whistle-blowing on my brother and that animal Oldfield. I posted them to Kent Farrell. What I expected to happen, I don't know. But anything to get that sick feeling out of my stomach.

What made it worse was — when I was saying goodbye to Keith in hospital, he whispered to me, 'You didn't tell them anything, did you?' So I said 'No' because that was what he wanted to hear. I didn't tell him what I was *going* to do. I'm beginning to realize there's more than one way of lying, *or telling the truth.*

So when that letter went in the post I felt better and worse at the same time. Understand? 'Course you do – 'cause you don't exist.

School was full of rumours and nods and nudges and funny looks. Some thought I was a hero. But some didn't, I could tell. One or two obviously thought Keith should have gone under the ice and stayed there. Rat told me there was a rumour we'd both tried to drown ourselves – a suicide pact. Where he gets these stories from I can't imagine.

The powers-that-be were keeping quiet. Sandy did not have the word with me he'd threatened to, but he said blush-making things to the class about me. I knew he was waiting for me to own up, but he knew better than keep on at me. I am actually getting to like old Sandeman.

I hadn't seen my brother for days. He was avoiding me at home and I hardly ever saw him at school anyway.

The one day the story ran round school like wildfire. Oldfield was expelled. It might be a police matter. My brother was suspended for three months. No big announcement in assembly. All low profile.

You can imagine how I felt. Kent Farrell must have understood my story and gone straight to the school. By the time I went home that day, I'd switched right from feeling angry with my brother to feeling sorry for him.

Once I was home and had dumped my gear I sneaked up to his room. Mother was busy with plates and cups in the kitchen. I tapped on his door. No answer. Inside all his stuff was gone (or put away), no papers, no clothes lying about. Father's pictures had vanished from the chest of drawers. My brother had left.

Quickly I went downstairs, forgetting to move quietly. I heard my mother call: 'That you, Gawain?' but by then I was slamming the front door and off down the road looking for a phonebox.

The first one was — you guessed it — out of order. I had to wander round what seemed like miles till I found one that worked. When I got through to the Curtisses Blossom answered, as I hoped she would.

'Hey, Blossom!' I don't know why I was whispering. 'Is my brother at your place... like living there?'

'No way. I don't think he and Big Sister have even talked to each other for a fortnight. Wherever he is, it's not here. Why?'

'Tell you some other time,' I promised, put the phone down and began to go home.

As I reached the street where I live I could see a taxi pulling away from our gate. I slowed down, stopped to get my breath back, then crept up our little garden path and slid the front door open as if I was going to rob the place.

Inside I stood in the passage and listened. Voices came from the lounge. The door was not closed. I could hear every word, because Grandmother had arrived. Both she and Mother speak very clearly. Mother sounded as if she was going to burst into tears.

'I can't take much more. I tried to accept I'd lost him, that he was dead, even though he was posted missing. I learned to live without him, but I didn't find anyone else. I don't say I never looked at other men. But I put them off.'

'I know,' said Grandmother.

My mother gave a funny sort of laugh. 'The fact is they all wanted to boss me and I won't have that.'

'I know, I know.'

'Then, just as at last I meet a human being, one who listens when I talk, treats me courteously, my husband writes to me. He's alive. He's been living in Argentina of all places. Not just a deserter, but probably a traitor as well, working for dictators.'

'Vivien,' said my grandmother. 'They're not dictators over there any more.'

'They were when he — went over.' My mother's voice got higher. 'But what do I do? He wants to know about the boys, photos and so on...

'Suppose he wants to come — home. There'll be a scandal, a trial or what. But I can't just reject him.

He's my husband.' She took a deep breath. 'Then if that weren't enough, there's this trouble at school, Lance involved in something awful, though he's got off lightly. He's just suspended. But what has he done? Joined the Army.'

'Surely you wanted him to?'

'Not just like that, not running from school. I wanted him to take his exams, and...'

'Maybe he saw it differently...'

The worst thing is, my mother wasn't listening. 'This business, it involved Gawain. He seems to have taken up with this older boy. I know Lance can be a bit hard on him, but...'

'Lancelot and Gawain,' said my grandmother. 'When you chose those names, did you remember that the originals, the knights, hated each other? And Gawain betrayed Lancelot...'

I wanted then to run upstairs, to my room and hide, but Grandmother went on: 'Vivien, have you talked to Gawain about any of this?'

'Oh, Gawain. He's very bright, but he's such a baby. Head always in a book. I can't talk to him.'

'I think you should try. Right now.'

'Gawain's not here.'

'But he is, listening outside the door, like his father used to.'

SYLVANIA QUEST

Gaw Penhallon

Chapter Fourteen
Return of the Sword

Without waiting for further invitation, Dearna raised his harp and struck a golden note. Then he began to sing of battles fought and won, of bold knights and fair ladies. The audience listened as the song went on. Only Tauro on his side of the hall seemed as though his patience might be tried.

Next Dearna began to sing of what he called 'Sylvania's Hope'. This was a sword called Exordo, now lost for ever in the heart of the land.

Now Tauro called out: 'Hurry and finish your song, minstrel.'

'It is nearly done, Majesty,' answered Dearna. 'I shall end my song with the tale of its loss.'

And in frozen silence he sang in a few short phrases of the murder of the priest Clarus amid the snowbound woods. There was a gasp of horror as he sang.

Sylva, her face pale, called out: 'Is the tale true, O minstrel?'

'It is, O Queen.'

'Who would do such a foul crime?'

'The man who wishes to marry you.'

There was a gasp of horror from the guests.

'Seize the minstrel,' roared Tauro, and a score of guards rushed forward. But at that same moment a score of men and women from among the spectators leapt out and surrounded Dearna.

Tauro waved back his guards. He smiled at the Queen. 'For your sake I will forgive this fool of a minstrel and his lying story. Let the wedding proceed and let him leave the palace before he is thrashed.'

'The story is no lie, Tauro,' called Ingawa. Thrusting aside the two guards he strode into the centre of the hall. 'I saw it happen. Tauro wanted the magic sword. But Clarus died to keep it from him. Now it is lost for ever.'

'Not so,' shouted Dearna. 'The sword is found. It is here, and by its might and the freedom of Sylvania shall be restored.'

As Dearna spoke these fateful words, one of the women standing around Dearna stepped forward. She tore off her gown and veil and stood in full armour. It was Blodwen. With a sweep of her arm, she held aloft Exordo.

'When Clarus knew he would soon die, he sought me out in the forest and gave me the sword. Now he is gone, it is mine to keep. I have taken up the fight that Ingawa began. And his brother Tancelo has joined my band. Tauro, you are doomed.'

Tauro's face twisted with rage as a score of men and women threw off their disguises to show themselves as armed fighters. Blodwen spoke again.

'Tauro, you are free to leave the citadel. And leave Sylvania within seven days. After that all Taurans in arms on our soil will die.'

Silently and followed by his minion, the tyrant left the hall. Sylva took her place on the throne. Then Blodwen spoke again.

'One last secret must be revealed. Throw off your disguise, Dearna. Reveal yourself as Anedar, the knight of Sylvania, who never died. Be reunited with your Queen, O minstrel warrior.'

The great hall rang with cheers and laughter.

THE END

English   The High School
<u>My Favourite Reading</u>   Bayfield, Oxon.

26th January

If this had been a few weeks ago, I should have been talking endlessly about the latest Terry Pratchett book. But at Christmas my grandmother gave me an old suitcase belonging to my father. Inside it were eight books.

They looked very old and worn. He must have read them to pieces when was my age. It is amazing just to think about it.

I will put down the names of the books, just as I found them. Some of them sound very strange.

Tschiffely's Ride, a man's journey on horseback along the Andes mountains.

The Rifle Rangers by Mayne Reid, a very old book about war in Mexico.

Westward Ho! by Charles Kingsley, another very old one, the story of an Elizabethan adventurer who rescues an Indian princess.

The Lost World by Arthur Conan Doyle. I'd seen the film, some scientists find living dinosaurs in South America.

Last and First Men by Olaf Stapledon, sort of futuristic – in Patagonia, pretty grim about wiping out civilization.

The Lighthouse at the End of the World by Jules Verne, about the far South, Cape Horn where all the storms are.

But the books which really interested me were the ones my father read most. The backs were almost falling off them and the pages were thumb-marked.

One was *Courts of the Morning* by John Buchan and the other was *Green Mansions* by W.H. Hudson.

The first looked very exciting and so it proved to be, though I was disappointed that it did not have much about Richard Hannay.

The other book was very strange, well, weird almost. My father had marked some pages in pencil.

These two I shall read very carefully because I think they may tell me something about my father.

22, Croxton
(For the time being)

28th January

Hi, at last.

I am not a fast reader. No one believes me, because I am a keen reader. So I am, but slow. It took me all one weekend to look through that suitcase full of books, of my father's, and read two of them properly.

I started with *Green Mansions* for two reasons. One was those pencil marks my father had made. I'd never dream of writing in a book. It must have been important to him.

The other reason was that the person telling the story right at the beginning is in Georgetown, Guyana, which is where my father was when he was my age. Maybe that is where he got the book.

The hero treks through the rain forest, hundreds of miles, rivers and snakes, Indians with poison darts, wild animals, till he meets an old man and a girl. She is called Rima and is like a spirit in the trees.

Where my father had marked was halfway through the book. The hero tried to show Rima what the world was like outside the jungle, using stones on the ground to mark the mountains and cities. I'll give you some of the bits.

'Bolivia, Peru, Chile ending at last in the south with Patagonia, a cold arid land, bleak and desolate... where earth ends and the Pacific Ocean begins...

'... the Cordilleras... that world-long stupendous chain... sea of Titicaca... the summits white with everlasting snows... the darkening tempest... the condor's flight... flame-breathing Cotopaxi, Chimborazo Antisana... Cuzco, the highest dwelling place of man on earth...

'East of the Andes, the rivers, what rivers, the green plains that are like the sea...'

My father must have been crazy about South America and choked when he had to leave it.

Then I read *Courts of the Morning* right through without stopping, which is going some, because it's nearly 500 pages. I waited till I was sure my mother was asleep at night, then put the light on to read more. Parts were a bit boring, parts were exciting when you got used to the way he writes.

But the most exciting thing was imagining why my father had read it so much. It wasn't long before I began to get it. The hero had been in the wars. He was around forty but still a bit like a kid, mad about South America, spoke some Spanish. It fitted my father because when he went missing in Argentina, he was almost forty.

The book's hero had gone back to South America to a made-up place, Olifa. He'd become a guerrilla to fight a dictator.

By Sunday afternoon I'd made up my mind about my father. He must have gone on that raid in the Falklands War intending never to come back. He wasn't deserting to help the Argentine dictators, but to fight them.

He was crazy, but he was for real. In some little ways he was — a bit like me. And there was nothing to be ashamed of in him, nothing.

I got so worked up about it, I almost ran down to talk to my mother, when I heard heavy footsteps, boots on the stairs. Peering out of my door I saw Brother going into his room. He was in army uniform, but not officer's.

When I saw him I ducked back. After shopping him (via Kent Farrell) I couldn't face him. On the other hand I wanted him to know about Father. So I sat down for a quick think, and made up a little speech, something like

'Lance. I'm sorry about what happened — about Keith. But it's all right about Father.'

Repeating it to myself gave me the nerve to go out of my room and knock on his door.

'Come,' he shouted, very military. I went in. He was sitting on the bed, wrapping up Father's picture, and his press cuttings in brown paper. I opened my mouth to make my speech when he looked up, grinned and banged on the bed with his fist, inviting me to sit down. I did and he said:

'Look, kid, I'm sorry about what happened with Keith. But it's all right about Father.'

I was gobsmacked. He didn't notice, but just went on talking. I listened.

'I don't know why I was so mad about Clarrie. Well, maybe I do. But I shouldn't have gone off and left him on the ice, after Oldie smashed his face.'

'You didn't know what would happen...'

'I should have done, kid. But what was worse, I kept quiet afterwards, hoping nobody would find out. When the two of you were in hospital, I couldn't admit I'd been involved. But it all came out later on.'

'Yes,' I began to say, 'I'm sor— '

But he wasn't listening.

'It was Helen. When Oldie and I didn't sign that 'get well' card for Clarrie she put two and two together and made five. We had this big row. "You're jealous about your kid brother," she said and "Wain's more of a man than you are."

'Then she said it was all off if I didn't own up. So I went to the Boss. I went to the hospital and grovelled to Keith. He hadn't said a word to anyone. That really got to me. Then I decided to join up, right away.'

'But, aren't you and Helen… again?'

He laughed. Well, he sort of barked. 'No way! I don't like being told what to do. Anyway it wouldn't work. We'd have split up sooner or later. And it got me off the hook about college. That was really Mother, wanting me to go higher up the tree than Father. But I'm going in the Army in my own way.'

'Lance!' I was almost bursting. 'About Father.' He listened while I told him about the books. At first he was baffled, then he began to nod.

'That was smart, our kid. You know, Mother's had another letter, yesterday. A long one, with the whole story. She was going to tell you today, after she told me.'

Then he said: 'He won't come back. It's too complicated. He thinks we'll be better off like we are. Just wanted to know we were OK. And… he found somebody over there.'

That was it, that was the other thing about *Green Mansions*.

English   The High School
<u>My Birthday</u>   Bayfield, Oxon.

15th February

Like the Royal Family, I spent this quietly at home. My friends, Blossom and Christopher and Graham, came round. My mother laid on lots of food and my friends noshed the lot. Well, I did quite well, too.

I got an encyclopaedia from my grandparents. There was a birthday card from my brother, who is doing his Army training in the wilds of Scotland. I think he hopes eventually to do United Nations work somewhere. There are lots of places which need it.

He kindly said I could have my father's cricket bat which was passed on to him, which is a nice thought, even if I shan't use it much, perhaps.

Now I must look forward to my thirteenth year. That sounds quite impressive. I read in a book somewhere that you pretend to be older until you get to a certain age and then you start pretending that you are younger than you really are. I cannot see myself getting to that age, somehow.

Still, I must move on. This is the time in life when you experience physical change and your voice begins to go funny and you start to shoot up or grow rapidly. I don't think I shall do the latter.

At this time of life you are also supposed to start understanding jokes with double meanings. If this is so, then it will come as a relief and I shall be able to laugh at the same time as other people rather than look baffled.

And you are supposed to start being rotten to the new people who start at school in the way older people were rotten to you when you started. But I hope I shall not do that.

My ambition in life is to survive.

I nearly forgot. On my birthday I also got a card from Kent Farrell, the author. He said he had read the Sylvania fantasy story I sent to him in the post. He thought it showed an advance on my previous work, but was not quite suitable for publication.

He says I must keep on writing and I shall.